FINDING HIMSELF AGAIN

~~ ~~

ANN M PRATLEY

BY ANN M PRATLEY

Chisholm Manor Series
Alessandra
Elizabeth

Suspense / Crime
Hoonigan
Resolution of Happiness
Home by the Sea
Tiger in Our House

Forbidden Conflicts Series
Amethyst of Youth
Ruby of Law
Diamond of War
Sapphire of Prejudice
Emerald of Wisdom

Freedom of Flight Series
Christian ~ Brandon ~ Trinity

ISBN- 978-1-99-116462-9

CHAPTER 1

Tom Santini sat in the park near Bondi Beach in Sydney, Australia, watching the sun slowly lower and begin to disappear. It had been six months since he'd been released from prison. Even though he'd been a free man for half a year, the simple scene of the sun going down seemed like a miracle he wondered if he'd ever get used to.

When he was eighteen, Tom had delivered a one-punch hit to another kid at an out of control party. The guy hadn't survived and Tom had been imprisoned for manslaughter for ten long years. When he'd finally been freed he'd felt the harshness of that reality. All he'd been trying to do was defend his friends from a gang who had invaded what should have been a quiet and laid back celebration of finishing high school.

Tom and his friends hadn't wanted or expected any trouble. Word of the party had spread and the house had been invaded by a rough group who definitely *were* looking for trouble. When one guy had tried to force himself on a close friend of Tom's, Tom had acted instinctively. He'd laid that last hand on him. It wasn't how he'd intended things to go. He'd just wanted the guy to back off, and for him and his friends to leave. Tom didn't know that one punch could result in things going as badly as they had. At that young age, he'd gone from fighting to protect his friends, to finding himself behind bars.

The time was now served. He was a free man again. Returning to the home of his parents hadn't been easy. They loved him; he knew that. His father's love was distant and almost unrecognizable. His mother's love suffocated him.

Sometimes it felt like too much, the contrast between the stark brutal existence inside prison and the infinite choices presented outside. He wanted to start a new life … a *better* life. But how could he do that when forever more he would be known as a man who'd killed someone?

Since his release, he'd been lucky. His brother, Graham, had been dating a woman who seemingly had been driving him crazy for months. Tessa Thompson had worked hard to become one of the best lawyers in the city. So had Graham. When they'd come up against each other on a case, sparks had instantly flown. Tessa had initially resisted the instant physical attraction to him but finally had given in. Anyone who saw them together knew they were meant to be together. The only two people who'd resisted the idea of them being a couple had been Graham and Tessa themselves. Now their initial craziness was behind them. They'd gotten married and were expecting a child together. Good on them. Tom felt no resentment toward his brother for finding happiness in love so easily when he'd been the one to run away from it his whole life.

If Tom was completely honest with himself, he had to admit that he was envious of what his brother had so easily found. For as long as he could remember, he had believed in love and he honestly thought he was meant to find it. He had wanted it before he'd made that life-altering mistake ten years earlier. He still held onto the hope that it could happen for him. But who would want a man who must be violent, to have been in prison for manslaughter for a decade?

Since he'd been freed, every few nights when the sky was clear and the air warm he found himself walking to the park three blocks from his parents' home. There he sat on a swing and idly moved back and forth with no great effort. Life in Australia was all that he'd ever known. He'd never seen the wondrous far off lands of any other country. He knew he had family in America but he'd only ever met one of them. Los Angeles seemed a distant and unreachable location to him. Now that he held the title of ex-criminal, Australia felt too small.

He had to sort his life out. He knew that. Graham and Tessa had helped with their encouragement. He was doing well in his job at Toby's Stop'n'Dine in the centre of the town. Before he'd gone to prison he'd had a few different after school and weekend jobs. He didn't care what he did now. He just needed to find a way to feel normal again. To feel *human* again. He was actually enjoying the work. The location of the café meant that it was within walking distance of large offices around the area. Slowly, he was beginning to recognize customers who came in at least a couple of times each week.

His boss, Toby, was amazing. Father to a daughter who was in prison for something he considered she shouldn't be, he was the perfect employer. He was eager to give Tom a chance, just as he hoped someone would give his little girl a chance when she was released from prison.

It wasn't broadcast that Tom had been in jail. Only a select few knew that. Regardless, he expected there would always be a chance that it would get out and people might react badly toward him. He hated the thought of that but he was a realist. Things got out. It was just the way of the world, especially with the wonderful invention of the Internet. Nothing was sacred anymore. If they wanted to, anyone could find out anything. It was just one of the things that had changed life outside during the dark years when he was inside.

He sat on the swing, watching the darkness close around him. He needed to go back to his parents' house. His mother needed him to be there but not for any reason other than for her to know that he was fine and he was safe. She suffocated him, yes, but she did it out of love. He needed to be honest with her so the two of them could start over again, with a relationship that was a bit more equal. A little bit less effort on her side. A little bit more on his. If they could only find that median, he was sure things would be better for both of them.

His brother, he didn't need to worry about. The two of them had shared a long history of not getting on but recent conversations had started to change that. The anger Tom had felt at Graham for not visiting him much in prison, had now been replaced with a greater level of understanding. He'd wanted to blame everyone else for everything but nothing had ever been anyone else's fault. That had been a copout to avoid taking responsibility for his own actions. A deflection. That was now behind him. The past was past. It was time to move forward… *really* move forward. It was time to not just say the words, but actually follow through with actions.

He stood, determined as a first step to get home at an hour that would put his mother's mind at rest. She still worried about him; overly so, but also reasonably so. It was an easy place to start, simply being home early enough each evening and staying home until he saw her first thing each morning. His café hours allowed for that. It was an easy thing to do, so long as he could keep his mind in a positive state and not drift back to the negative.

It was a short walk back to the house where they lived. He didn't want to live with his parents for an extended period of time but he'd stay with them for the moment, at least until he felt his mother was at ease with who he was now. Until she truly believed he had started living once more. Until she had faith that he wouldn't do anything stupid again that would send him back to prison. He knew that was one of her fears but he had no intention of ever going back there. None whatsoever.

He walked into the house and sought her out immediately. It was easy to see the relief on her face as she moved to jump up and start making a fuss. He didn't expect his father to be home. He hardly ever was.

"Just sit and relax and let me get you something, Mom. How about a nice cup of tea or coffee?"

Victoria quietly sat back in the seat she'd been in when she'd heard him come in. She didn't want to do anything to upset him and make him want to leave so she nodded and replied quietly. "A cup of tea would be nice."

Tom made and brought the tea to her. As he put the cup down on the table beside her, he leaned over and kissed her forehead.

"Don't worry about me so much. I'm here now and I'll be staying in all night, so don't wait up, worrying. I'm heading off to bed and I will see you in the morning. Alright?"

He saw her nod in surprise of his calmness and consideration. He knew he had a long way to go to start to put everyone at ease so they would stop worrying about him. It didn't matter how long that took. He would succeed in doing it.

Glancing back at her before he left the room, he saw she was more relaxed than she had been only minutes earlier when he'd arrived. It felt good to know that he'd helped with her change in her level of fear. It would be nicer if his father would step up and also give her some attention now and then, but after years of neglect, that was unlikely to change now.

CHAPTER 2

The next morning Tom was woken by the sound of the digital alarm clock next to him. Reaching over and slamming the alarm off, he became aware of the sound of rain falling heavily on the roof. The sound was reassuring. It was a sound he'd missed in prison, never being close enough to the roof to hear the rain. Much of the time he hadn't known what was happening outside at all.

He let himself lie still for a few minutes, just listening. There was so much to readjust to in the outside world. The sound of rain was just one of the many things that he hadn't even thought about before. So much he'd taken for granted when he was younger. He would never again fail to fully appreciate the simple aspects of life.

After lengthy contemplation, he dragged himself from his bed. It had felt like a chore the first few days but he was now getting used to it. He slipped on his clothes and made his way down the hallway to the bathroom. There he locked the door and turned on the shower. As the water slowly heated he removed all of his clothing and stood in front of the mirror. His body was different from what it had been when he'd first gone into prison. Then he'd been bulky and in the beginnings of shedding his teenage body and becoming muscular. In prison, his shape had changed. He was well toned and he liked the abs that were clearly visible, but he did want to put on a bit of weight. That, he knew, would come from being able to eat good food once again.

Steam started to approach him from the shower. He tested the water temperature with his hand before climbing under the spray. Closing his eyes, he let the water pound onto his back. Being able to shower with full belief that he was alone and he was safe was one more thing he wanted to maintain an appreciation for. He'd always taken things for granted. Now he wanted to keep things in the forefront of his mind as reasons to appreciate everything he had.

After showering, shaving and dressing again he made his way to the kitchen and put on a pot of coffee to brew. Bread in the toaster, he walked to the front door and reached out to pick up the morning newspaper that had been delivered. By the time his mother had gotten up, he was about to head out the door, ready for protection from the rain with his coat and scarf on.

"I have to get to work. Have a good day," he said and kissed her on the forehead before he ran out the door, eager to get on with the day.

Walking in the rain felt good to him. He

remembered how people used to always complain when it was a rainy day but the feeling of the drops hitting his head felt invigorating.

He reached the café and quickly opened, entered, and closed the door behind him.

"The sky's opening up today," said his boss, Toby. "Go out the back and hang your coat and scarf up to dry, Tom. It could be a quiet day today. On days like this people never come out in the same numbers as they do when the sun shines."

Tom moved to the back of the café, hung up his coat and then checked in with Toby to find out what prep he needed to give priority to. Silently but with determination, he got on with the job. It wasn't everyone's dream job but he was enjoying it.

"Tom, can you work out here and watch the front?" Toby asked. "I want to go through some of the deliveries that just came in so I'll be out back for a while. If you can watch out for customers, I'd appreciate it. Just holler if you need me."

The two men swapped places and Tom took note of where the fillings were set out. It was something he had to map out in his brain and each day he remembered it a bit better. He still had a ways to go before he would be able to instinctively reach for each of the fillings customers requested in their sandwiches and salad rolls.

Hearing the bell over the door sound, he looked up to see a woman walking in, absolutely soaked. It wasn't lost on Tom that her dress was wet enough to not only cling to her shapely form, but also reveal slightly more than he expected she would want it to.

Sensing someone looking at her, the woman looked up and her eye caught his. He gulped. The combination of her enticing body and the beauty of her face made him catch his breath. The more he looked at her, the more he knew he couldn't let her continue to walk around like she was; not without at least making sure she was aware of it.

He called out to Toby in the back. "Hey, Toby! Can you pass me my scarf from that hook there?" he asked and immediately caught it as it was thrown at him. "Thanks."

Tom watched as the woman walked up to the counter and began studying the large menu board. At the same time, though, she seemed to be looking at him just out of the very corner of her eye. Finally, she turned and faced him straight on.

"I'm sorry. I don't yet know what I want to order," she said, her voice sounding like the smoothest, most beautiful voice he'd ever heard.

"Take your time. But..." Tom started to say before experiencing doubt. Would she appreciate him pointing such a thing out? She might slap him and then what would Toby think?

"Yes?" the woman prompted.

"I … I want to say something to you but I don't want to risk you taking it as any kind of offense."

She looked at him as if surprised by his words but finally called him out on what he had been going to say.

"Then I promise not to take offense," she said, a sliver of amusement evident in her voice. "What did you want to tell me?"

Tom felt tongue-tied and didn't want to offend her. His discomfort was offset by not wanting her to walk around like that if she didn't know what people could see.

The woman saw him look around him, presumably taking care to not let anyone else hear.

"Your dress is very wet," he said, making her laugh.

"In case you hadn't noticed, it's pouring out there," she replied.

"Your dress is now see-through," Tom said as he pointed. "*Very* see-through."

He saw the woman's face change as she looked down in horror. She probably couldn't even see the vision she presented, from the angle she was looking. When she finally looked up at him, he could tell she'd finally comprehended what he'd said.

"I don't know..." she started to say as she wrapped her arm around herself to cover her breasts. She remembered that she'd worn one of her sexier bras that morning, simply because she loved how it felt. She also knew that it was flimsy material, and suspected that it wasn't doing anything to hide her breasts ... or worse, her nipples. "I don't know what to do..."

Tom picked up his scarf, shook it out to show her just how wide it opened up to, and signaled to her to step closer. When she did, he carefully wrapped it around her shoulders and secured it in front so that it hid everything that had previously been on show.

"There. Nothing can be seen now," he said, his hands remaining on the scarf for the moment. He knew he should move away but for just a moment he felt like he should stay right where he was. Closeness to a woman was something he hadn't experienced in a very long time.

"Thank you," she said. The words escaped her kissable mouth as if she had breathed them rather than said them.

Aware of how unprofessional his distance to her was, Tom took a step back and resumed his usual stance behind the counter.

"You are very welcome," he said. "Now, what deliciousness can we prepare for you today? I can make you a sandwich or salad roll with whatever fillings you desire, or I do make a mean smoothie."

The woman looked at him as if surprised by something about him. Over six feet tall with dark hair and dark brown eyes, he had always stood out in a crowd, ever since his growth spurt in school.

The stare became so intense that he found himself amused. He pointed one finger up at the board on the wall behind him.

As if the finger rising was a signal, the woman found herself broken out of the trance she had been in. She didn't know why but she was drawn to look at the man who had helped her. The simple act of offering a scarf to cover her revealing state was something she wasn't sure all men would do. She wasn't even sure that most men *would* do it. Wouldn't they rather keep staring, enjoying looking at a woman's body in that state, rather than help her to hide it?

She redirected her view and selected an item from the board. She wasn't really hungry. The rain had driven her to step into the first door that was close to her when the heaviness of it had intruded on her morning. The first item on the menu seemed fine. Looking briefly out the window, she cursed herself inwardly for not checking the weather report.

"It's really coming down out there," she heard the deep voice say from behind the counter.

When she turned back to him she saw him moving his hands deftly in creating the sandwich she had ordered. Even his hands looked sexy.

She pulled the scarf tighter around her, not wanting to let him see that he might have affected her physically. Trying to create a look of confidence on her face, she met his gaze.

"Yes," she replied. "I should have checked the weather forecast before I went out this morning."

Tom watched her with discreet glances as he built the creation. He was new to sandwich making, having only moved from just being the cashier to also helping in the food preparation over the previous few days. Surprising to him, he'd found it suited his creative side. Toby was sometimes strict about how much filling to put in each sandwich, but Tom snuck in an extra piece of bacon for good measure. Just this one time. She was cold and wet, after all. Why not let her enjoy her sandwich just that little bit more if he could?

"Is this to eat here or would you like it to go?" Tom asked her, his eyes never leaving her for very long.

She looked out the window again and sighed. The scarf was nice and even warming to her but she would have to step outside again without it. Seeing the way the rain was heavily coming down, she groaned. She didn't want to stand still for too long. Why had she worn a dress anyway?

She wanted to blend in and not been seen. She wanted to be invisible but for some reason that morning she had just wanted to feel normal. Wearing a dress and sexy lingerie helped with that. It made no sense that it did, but it still did regardless.

Tom saw her attention return to him.

"I think I will eat here," she said. "Just until it stops raining."

He laughed softly, with a distinctive gleam in his eye. "I think that could be quite a while."

He rang up the order and watched as she thanked him, took her food and sat as far away from the window as she could. She was facing it but he was savvy enough to see that she wanted to see, but not be seen. It was obvious to him that she might be trying to avoid someone. He'd been there before, many times in jail. He knew the signs.

Determined to not get involved, he grabbed the table cleaning cloth and began running it over each table, one by one. When he neared her, he heard her speak again.

"This really is delicious. You make good sandwiches!" she exclaimed. For the first time since she'd walked into the café, her voice sounded full of animation.

"I aim to please," he said and saw her blush. He was teasing her but instantly he wished he hadn't.

She didn't know him. He didn't want to sound like a player. That was something he definitely wasn't. He never had been. He'd never had time to grow and become one, even if it had been in his nature. No, deep inside of him there was a longing for love. He'd never loved before, and since being in prison he had wondered if he would ever love or be loved in return. He longed for that. He'd seen the way his brother Graham looked at Tessa. That was what he'd always wanted. There was irony that Graham never had.

He heard the door open and saw the person he was thinking about entering.

"What are you doing here?" he asked Graham as the door was closed and the sound of rain softened once more. Just turned thirty, with jet black hair and brown eyes, Graham was slightly shorter than his younger brother. As a man, though, he had a strong presence.

"I came to get a smoothie," Graham said. His voice revealed his usual brotherly sarcasm, as if that were the *obvious* reason he would be in the café.

Tom rolled his eyes at his brother but moved behind the counter.

"Which one do you want to try today?"

"I'll go with that Very Berry Blast one," Graham replied as he nodded and pointed at the menu board.

Tom smiled. "You've taken on Tessa's preferences already, I see," he teased his brother and saw a smile appear.

It was only recently the brothers had finally found a place in their relationship that enabled them to relax around each other. There had been many years during which things hadn't felt right. Tessa stepping in and having a harsh word to each of them had helped the mending process begin. It would still be a long road to full recovery for Tom's family, but he knew they were well on their way. Well, for him, his brother and his mother anyway. His father had stepped out of the loop long ago, even though he pretended on occasion to still be part of the family.

"To go?" Tom asked as he added a sinful spoonful of whipped cream onto the top of the smoothie.

"Yes," Graham replied. "I have to head to Brisbane for a few days so this is for the trek to the airport."

"Brisbane? What's there?" Tom asked, curious.

"Just some tidying up that I have to do."

Tom looked at his brother, wondering if he was keeping something under wraps.

"Is Tessa going with you?" he asked.

"No," Graham said. "She has too much work on right now so is staying here."

"Aww. The lovers' first break apart," Tom said

and Graham smiled in friendly frustration at him. Two years apart in age, they'd never much smiled in each other's presence in the past. Slowly, it was starting to happen, more and more. "No surfing for a while then."

The two of them had recently taken out their boards together for the first time since before Tom had gone to prison. It was an experiment on Graham's part, to see if he could wake his brother up from the ongoing depressed state he'd seemed to be in. Surfing had certainly helped.

"No, but definitely when I get back?" Graham asked as he started to turn to leave.

"Sure thing," Tom said as he grinned. "Good luck in Brisbane."

"Thanks, Tom."

After his brother had left, Tom turned back to look at the young woman. She was still eating her sandwich, now taking nibbles as if to make it last. For a moment he let himself believe that perhaps she was purposely taking her time so that she could enjoy his charm a little longer. Then he conceded she was probably trying to just put off going out in the rain.

Finally, she stood and approached him, unwrapping the scarf as she did.

"Thank you for this," she said, her gaze seeming to fly over his facial features. He had to admit it to himself; he liked her looking at him like that. No doubt about it.

"Keep it," he said, smiling at her.

"I can't…"

Tom shook his head and held up his hand as if to stop her from speaking.

"It's still pouring out there and even *that* isn't going to keep you dry, but it can at least keep you a little more hidden," he said. "Please, I insist. Take it. If you want to drop it back here another time, do, but if you don't, that's okay too."

The woman nodded and Tom saw a small, sad smile grace her face.

"Thank you," she said. "I really might not be able to bring it back…"

"Think nothing more of it. I wish I could help you more."

Nothing more was said as he watched her artfully rewrap the scarf so that it not only covered her shoulders and chest but also wove around her head like a hood. After she stepped out he saw her walk past the window before she disappeared from view.

Tom's mind remained on the woman for a few more minutes. He was intrigued by her. She had secrets, he was sure, but who was she? And how would he see her again?

The sound of the door opening broke him out of his thoughts and he was instantly caught up in serving another customer. He gave no more thought to the woman who had provided him with intrigue and quite a view.

~ ~ ~

Later in the afternoon, he looked up as the door opened. It was a pleasure to see Tessa entering. The rain had finally stopped and he could see through the window that a glimmer of sunshine was trying to push its way through the hovering clouds.

"Tessa. It's good to see you," Tom said. He meant it. When they had first been introduced by Graham, he hadn't been sure what to think of her but she had grown on him. She had a fire inside of her, and a level of determination that he could only admire. "What can we get you today?"

Right then, hearing the mention of Tessa's name, Toby came out front and greeted her also. With Tessa being one of his most loyal and favorite customers, he took great pride in making her salad rolls exactly as she liked them. Tom stood back and let the artist create.

"Have you seen Graham?" she asked Tom, surprising him.

"He was in here earlier," Tom replied. "Said he was flying to Brisbane."

Tessa showed a blank look on her face but said nothing. At that moment the door opened and Tom saw the woman from that morning coming in. She had dressed more for the day, now wearing jeans and a hoodie that certainly covered her far more than her dress had earlier. She first seemed to focus on him but then her eyes fell to someone else.

"Cat!" Tessa called out as she saw who had come into the café. "How wonderful to see you! It has been too many years! Where have you *been?*"

Tom watched the interaction and wondered if there was anyone on the planet that Tessa didn't know. His brother had told him she knew everybody but Tom had assumed that was some kind of exaggeration. Now he wondered if it was.

The young woman looked flustered, for a moment giving Tom the impression that she might have hoped to not see anyone she knew. She quickly covered it up, her face breaking out in what Tom believed was a fake smile.

"Tessa!" she exclaimed. "It *has* been a long time. How have you been?" she asked, avoiding the question that had been asked of her.

The two women hugged before Tessa turned back to Tom to pay for her lunch. When she'd done so, she turned to Cat once more.

"Do you want to sit down and catch up?"

"Oh, no, thank you, Tessa. I actually just came in to return this," Cat said, approaching the counter and handing the scarf to Tom. "This gentleman was very kind in lending it to me earlier today when I seemingly needed it."

Tom looked into her eyes and saw the slightest glimmer of amusement in them as she looked at him. He wondered if it was the result of her having seen in the mirror what he'd seen when she'd first walked in the door. At that thought, he felt his body react in a way he really didn't want it to at that moment. He leaned forward so that the counter would hide any evidence of his thinking about the vision of her in her wet dress. The image that was flashing before his eyes in his mind was causing a harsh reaction.

"Thank you," Cat said, breaking him from his thoughts.

"You are very welcome," he replied, unaware that his voice had dropped an octave or two and had taken on a slight husky sound to it.

Cat looked at him a moment longer. It surprised her to realize she was wondering what his full lips would be like to kiss.

"Well, how about a catch up another time?" they both heard Tessa's voice say from behind Cat.

"I…" Cat stuttered, taken aback by the question. She'd hoped to pass through her old town without really seeing or being noticed by anyone. "Actually, I'm not staying in town. I'm just passing through for the day."

Tessa felt a slight sadness that her old friend from high school didn't seem interested in the two of them talking. But more than that, she felt like something was definitely up with her.

"Okay," she replied.

Cat looked at her old school friend briefly before smiling sadly, giving one more smile at Tom, and then walking out.

"She's got secrets," Tom said.

Tessa wasn't sure if he'd meant to say it out loud but she agreed. "I think so too."

"Who is she?"

"She is Cat Cullen," Tessa said. "We went to high school together."

"I bet she was the popular high school beauty," Tom said. His voice sounded wistful and made Tessa laugh out loud.

"She was the school nerd," she said.

Tom was stunned into silence. Tessa smiled, said goodbye and left him like that.

~ ~ ~

The rest of the day passed without anything eventful happening. Now and then, thoughts of Cat Cullen would enter Tom's mind. He didn't want to think about her, especially since he knew she would have already left town. His desire to not think about her didn't quite happen in reality.

At closing time he took his time putting all the foodstuffs into the right cold storage, then swept and mopped the floors. Everything seemed to be moving slower all of a sudden.

"Go home, Tom," he heard Toby call out as he appeared from the back of the café. "I'll lock up soon. Go home and I'll see you in the morning. Thanks for another great day's work."

Tom put the broom, mop and bucket away and began his journey home. Having already started receiving pay for his work, he finally had money of his own. He thought about his mother on the way home. His father had gone out of town on work. Understanding his mother might miss him and Graham once she knew they were both out of town for a few days at least, Tom stopped by the local Chinese takeaway. His mother loved fried rice; *raved* about the stuff. It would be a nice treat for her.

When he walked into their home he found her on the sofa, unmoving with her eyes closed. Her stillness made Tom panic, instantly thinking the worst. As he started to shake her, she woke up. Tom was relieved she had only been asleep.

"Mom, I thought…" he started to say.

His mother laughed a little at him. "You thought I'd kicked the bucket? You don't know me at all, do you," she teased. "I'll be here … *forever*."

He knew she was trying to make light of his previous moment of distress so he let her hear a little chuckle from him in return. In Tom's earlier years, after his father had started being absent almost all of the time, the times when his mother had been depressed had driven Tom to be the one to use humor to try and lighten things. Now that he, Graham and his mother were all trying to work on their relationships together, he enjoyed seeing a little bit more of her humor come out now and then. His father came and went. His work took him all over the UK and he was away more than he was ever at home. For as long as Tom could remember, in their home it had always felt more like a three-person family than a four-person one.

"I picked up fried rice," Tom said, smiling at her. "I'll get plates. Stay where you are."

"Yes, bossy," his mother replied.

She pretended to not be so grateful to him but she was. She'd always been proud of him, even though he'd gone to jail. Even in that, she knew the truth. She knew he'd punched someone once without any intention to even really hurt the guy, let alone kill him. He'd just wanted to scare him enough to make him and his friends leave the party they were at, and to stop something bad happening to one of his female friends.

It had been a long time when Tom had been away. For his mother, time had seemed to slow and almost stop but now he was home. It had been rocky at the start, especially with the friction between her two sons, but now things seemed to be evening out. It was almost like all three of them were starting over.

When Tom came back into the room, he set the forks and plates on the table and started dishing out the rice meal.

"Have you seen your brother today?" his mother asked.

Tom nodded. "He came into the café this morning. Said he was heading to Brisbane for a few days for work."

"Why would he be going there for work?"

He handed a plate and fork to her and saw her take them with hunger visible on her face.

"I didn't ask," he replied. "But I don't think he'd want to be away from Tessa if he had no real reason to go."

They sat together and chatted about things that had happened in the world that day. His mother read the newspaper religiously every day. That made Tom happy. It gave them something to talk about other than just him, her and Graham.

When he climbed into bed later that night, he realized briefly before he went to sleep that it was the first day in literally years that the night of horror of ten years ago, hadn't entered his mind once all day. After years of it being at the forefront of his thoughts all day every day, it was only now, as he began to drift off to sleep, that he gave brief thought to it.

The realization made him smile. Maybe he was getting over it after all.

Moving on, getting over it and starting again.

That was, indeed, something to smile about.

CHAPTER 3

The next day at work, Tom flew through all that he had to. He had been brilliant at the till from the moment he'd started working there. Since then, Toby had taken time to train him in smoothie making and the art of sandwich making 'Toby style' and he was becoming good at that too. The reality was that he was loving working. Although some people might object to doing such a job, he appreciated every single moment that he was given to prove himself as a valuable and trustworthy employee. He could have been thinking ahead to another job down the line but he was happy where he was. Just being able to do a hard day's work, really meant something.

It was the last day of the working week for him, and it was a busy one. He loved the work when it was quiet or busy but his adrenaline flowed when there was a line of people waiting. Then he felt like he could do anything, as he worked under the pressure that he actually thrived on.

At the end of the day, Toby once again thanked him and affectionately told him to get out and not come back for two days. Tom smiled at his boss and walked out. He didn't have plans for his two days off but in the back of his mind was a quiet determination to use the time to get back into surfing again. He could say that it was just to increase his skill in it again. A more honest reason was that he wanted to be better than Graham the next time they went out together. That would annoy Graham no end. The thought made Tom smile. He wasn't serious in competing with his brother but if he could be just that little bit better the next time they took their boards out, it could be a laugh to see his brother's face.

That evening he took his mother to see a movie at the cinema. She hardly ever left the house anymore even though Tom kept trying to get her interested in things away from the home. He just had to find the right hobby or interest and surely he could get her to start at least going to some kind of club or something. Even just one afternoon a week would be a start.

She showed reluctance at the idea of going out to see a movie, but inside she was glowing. He was a good kid to do such a thing. She knew he worried about her. Both of her sons did and she did want to give them less to worry about. The contrast between what she thought was right for her, and what she thought was right for them, seemed sometimes too great. The two extremes were too far apart but she would keep trying. Graham had tried hard to mend things with his brother. Tom was trying hard to get a normal life back. It was only fair that she do her bit to change some things in her life too, to give her sons peace. Her husband - well, he just wasn't worth thinking about.

The movie was a historical romance. It wasn't Tom's taste at all, but he felt better taking his mother to that than taking her to see a bloodthirsty horror or an erotic thriller with plenty of 'adult content' warnings. Once they were settled he resigned himself. When they exited the theatre after the credits rolled up, he spoke as enthusiastically about the storyline as his mother did. It was a nice evening. Although she wouldn't say it, he did believe that his mother enjoyed it too. It was a start.

~ ~ ~

The following morning, Tom woke to the feeling of sunshine warming his face. It was a welcome change from the blaring alarm that had woken him on previous mornings. The room wasn't completely light. The curtains did keep some light out but they were just sheer enough to let the warmth flow through.

Tom smiled to himself. He was going surfing. His brother would probably be annoyed when he returned home, but Tom was going anyway. Graham had been the one to nudge him to get back into it, albeit at Tessa's suggestion. Now he was going to follow their encouragement and enjoy it.

After a quick shower and breakfast, he grabbed his board from the shed in the yard and headed down to the beach. Once there, he stood for a long while at the top edge of the sand and just looked. The waves looked good; not great, but they were definitely there. The feeling of a mild breeze blowing across his face helped to calm his adrenaline. He closed his eyes and focused on breathing in the salty air before opening them again and starting to make his way across the sand.

Wetsuit on, he ventured into the water. It was a shock with the temperature as cold as it was, but he endured it. He knew he would soon be able to ignore it. He climbed onto his board and paddled out as far as he dared go, before turning and waiting. When the first wave came that he could see would suit his desires, he prepared and then rode it. He did it over and over until finally, he could see the tide changing.

Running back into shore, he felt a reluctance but also exhilaration. He was about to sit down on the sand and just watch the waves when out of the corner of his eye he saw a young woman sitting on a large rock far off to his right. It was too far to be sure, but he thought she looked similar to the woman he'd seen in the café earlier that week.

Cat. Tessa had said her last name but he struggled with it now. Cat … Rogers? No … Callahan? No! Cullen? Cat Cullen? Yes! That was it.

He watched her for a long while, wondering if it *was* her. Even if it wasn't, could he go and say hello to whoever it was? She seemed to be deep in thought. Perhaps he could do a good deed and provide a shoulder and an ear.

Once his mind was made up, he began walking swiftly in that direction. He kept an eye on the woman, still wondering if it could be her. She maintained her focus straight ahead in the direction of the ocean. Tom wondered if, behind her sunglasses, she might have her eyes closed because she didn't move her head in his direction at all.

When he reached her, he still couldn't be sure it was her, with her eyes covered like they were. He decided to take the plunge and dive right in.

"Hello," he said. As soon as he said it, the head moved to his direction and he saw her mouth make the shape of an 'o' as if she were startled.

She said nothing for a long time, but finally removed her sunglasses and allowed him to see her. He was pleased to see that she was letting him know that it was her.

"Oh … umm … hi," she seemed to stutter out. Her aura gave off an impression of guilt as if she had been caught in the act of doing something she shouldn't.

"I don't think you will have forgotten me so soon," Tom replied, with a slight tease in his voice.

Cat shook her head. No indeed, she said to herself in her thoughts. She certainly did not say those words out loud. Finally, Tom saw her smile.

"How could I forget my rainy day savior who saved me from extreme embarrassment?" she teased and saw Tom smile in response.

For the first time in a long while, Cat felt arousal in her body. She knew he wasn't even doing anything to inspire it but the look of him with his hair wet and messy around his face, and the smile he was giving her, was making her want to melt.

"Can I sit with you?" Tom ventured to ask, fully anticipating a rejection. He was wrong to assume that would happen, as she nodded and moved over slightly. The rock was large with a flat top surface. Tom wedged his board into the sand and then climbed up to settle beside her. "I thought you were only passing through town."

Cat let out a sigh of resignation. She'd forgotten how small the area could be despite its not-so-small population. She dreamed of starting over in a new life, away from recent stresses, but she'd made a mistake coming home. It just wasn't possible to start over in a previous hometown.

"I actually live here," she said. "I wasn't honest with Tessa when I saw her."

"Why?"

He heard her laugh quietly. It sounded not like a laugh so much as an expression of sarcasm.

"When I was in high school, I was always picked on by other kids," she said. "I wasn't sporty, I wasn't creative or musical, and I was good at math. *Really* good. Tessa, and the other kids in her family, were the popular kids."

"I got the impression from Tessa that you two had been friends," Tom replied.

"No, not really. Maybe she remembers it that way. I remember it differently."

He looked at her, appreciative that she had left her sunglasses propped up on top of her head so he could see her eyes as she spoke.

"Why would your school years make you act like you were friends with her when you came into the café the other day?"

"Oh, well, she was enthusiastic, and I never had anything against Tessa," Cat said. "I thought she was one of the nicer popular kids. To be honest, I've done things that I'm not proud of, and talking to people from my past … I don't know. I guess I don't want to have to explain how my life has changed."

Cat saw Tom nod as he continued to look into her eyes.

"I can relate to that completely," he said.

"You can?"

"Oh, yeah. Everything seems too hard in high school and then we leave and there are so many expectations," Tom said. "We make choices. Some of them turn out to be really bad ones and then it can feel like there's no way back to being seen as the good person you were before you made that mistake."

Cat heard the words and couldn't believe how spot-on he was to how she felt some days. *Most* days.

"Yes! That's it exactly!" she exclaimed.

"But that doesn't explain why you said you were just passing through," Tom said quietly.

"I thought that I could just get through seeing her and let her think I was doing okay and we would never see each other again," Cat replied.

They sat in silence for a while before Tom spoke again.

"Are you not okay, Cat?" he asked.

She liked him saying her name. The deepness of it seemed to surge through her, connecting to a part of her that had been asleep for quite a while. On the tip of her tongue were two words, wanting to scream out of her. 'Kiss me!' She held back from letting the two words out. What kind of thought was that?!

"I'm okay," she instead said. "Compared to

many people, I am more than okay. I just want to start over, somewhere, somehow."

"What are you running from?"

"Oh, you don't want to know that, I am sure."

He frowned at her. "I think I do - if you want to talk to me about it, that is."

Cat sat in silence, assembling words in her head before she let the words start to flow.

"I was in a relationship that didn't end well," she began. "He cheated on me and I found it quite easy to leave. We had been living together but when I found out about what he'd been doing, I just threw together what I could into a suitcase and left. I didn't care about the big stuff. I just grabbed my clothes, essentials and sentimental things, and jumped in my car."

"And?" Tom pressed.

"When he realized I was gone, he came after me. He found me at a friend's house, and forced his way in there," she said. "I had to call the cops and I got a restraining order taken out on him. I don't even know why he was wanting to see me. He's got someone new…"

"Maybe it was more about controlling you, than being with you."

Cat pondered that and wondered if that could be the case. She had tried to figure things out since the day she had left. That very day he had started to follow her. It made no sense that he would want to be with her. If that were the case, why did he sleep with at least one other woman?

"Perhaps you're right. I don't know," she said.

"What has happened since then? Are you free now?" he asked, suddenly feeling a slight protectiveness come over him. He didn't really want to feel that. That was what had driven him to take action once before - action that had ended up with him going to jail. But at the same time, he couldn't just accept a woman being harassed either.

"Sometimes I think I'm okay," Cat replied. "Other times I feel like maybe someone is following me. I can't be sure. It has been four weeks since I actually saw him, so he could have given up. I *hope* he's given up."

The conversation had taken Tom back to another situation. That seemed like a lifetime ago. He'd learned the hard way how one small choice could make such a large effect on a life. Like one tiny raindrop hitting a bowl of water and the ripples growing and gathering momentum until they seemed like large waves.

"Have you got somewhere safe to stay?" Tom asked her, a feeling of dread falling over him.

"I do," Cat said. "A friend has let me stay in her home near here."

"And does he know your friend?" Tom asked and saw her shake her head in response.

"No," Cat replied. "I arranged this through a friend of a friend so he couldn't see where I am through messages or anything like that."

They were both silent for a while before she looked closely at his face and wondered what he was thinking of her.

As if already aware of her question, Tom spoke. "I can't get the image of you in that wet dress out of my mind."

He looked at her and saw her blush, but the blush was accompanied by a smile.

"I don't know what to say to that," she then said, laughing softly.

Tom grinned at her. "You don't have to say anything. I just thought I'd let you know."

"When I got back to the house, I did look in the mirror. I was more than a little bit horrified that people had seen me like that," she said, grinning and blushing at the same time. "Thank you for giving me your scarf."

"Hmm," he started to respond softly. "I actually quite liked how you looked. As I said, the image is still in my mind … and it's an image I like."

"But you helped me cover up."

He nodded. "Yeah, of course! Just because you looked good to me, didn't make me think you were intentionally going around town looking like that. But it *was* a good look…"

Cat giggled out loud, suddenly feeling the

happiest she had in a long while. She let herself enjoy it and showed her enjoyment by lightly punching his arm. It felt so easy between them, almost as if they had been friends for a long time. But they had only just met.

"What is *your* story? Wait, what is your *name?*" she asked him and immediately saw him close up before her eyes.

"I'm Tom," he said, holding out one hand to shake hers even though he didn't really want to talk about himself.

"And?" Cat pushed. "What secrets are you holding, Tom? I can tell that you are."

Tom pulled his hand back and looked out over the sea once more. This was the kind of situation he had thought he should avoid but if he kept doing that, would he ever be able to let anyone into his life again? He proceeded, albeit with caution.

"I do have secrets, Cat," he said quietly. "I have made my share of mistakes, and I've paid a price for that. I, too, dream of starting over in a new life. Doing it isn't as easy as wishing it but slowly I'm getting things in order."

"What would you do, if you had the choice to do anything?" Cat asked, curious.

"Hmm, well, a while back I got to meet a distant American cousin, Cameron, when he came to Australia to see our mutual cousin, Daniel," he said. "Apparently I have a lot of cousins in the US. I do like the thought of flying to a far off land and starting over as a completely new person."

"And can you?"

"I looked into it when I first got … when I first *thought* about it. There were some considerations that made me think that I might not be allowed to live and work there," he replied. "I don't know … after looking into it, it all seemed a bit too hard. I decided then that I'd stay here and just try and make a better go of it. There are things I need to get over and things I want to improve about myself. The past has to be left in the past. Running away to Los Angeles wouldn't really change anything. It would just be a sticking plaster over a deep wound."

Cat considered his words before she continued the conversation. "Well, I won't ask you any more about that. This chat has become too serious anyway, right? Tell me about your surfing."

"Were you watching me?" he asked, making her blush again.

"I quite liked how you looked," she said and after a moment heard him laugh loudly as he realized she had thrown his words right back at him.

"Ahh, well, it is something I enjoyed when I was in high school and am only now beginning to try to get into it again," Tom said. "It's nice being out there. I get a feeling of freedom and peace when I'm on the water. It's good for me."

Cat nodded. "I can see that being out there would be a very peaceful place to be. Like hiding from the world for a few hours, somewhere that no-one else can harass or question."

"Yes," he said and then looked at her as a light bulb moment happened in his thoughts. "Have you surfed before?"

"Me? No!" Cat exclaimed. "But I have always thought it must be an invigorating and freeing activity to do."

"Would you like to learn?" he asked and saw her give him a look of surprise.

"I don't know. Are you offering to teach me?"

He nodded. "If you like. I only have today and tomorrow off work and then I won't be surfing again till next week. But I have another board and I'd be happy to take you out. I have a wetsuit, although it might be a bit big…"

"Are you serious?" she asked as she felt adrenaline flow through her at the idea.

"Yes, of course. What do you think?"

"I … I don't know. You've taken me by surprise."

"Well, let's make it an open invitation," Tom said. "If you want me to teach you, I'll see you here tomorrow morning. If you don't, then you won't be here. How's that? No pressure whatsoever."

Cat nodded. For the moment she felt a little like she had before everything had gone bad with Tony. Like there was no reason to be stressed all the time, or in fear.

"Are you hungry?" she asked, completely out of the blue.

"I can always eat," Tom said, grinning. "What did you have in mind?"

"The house I'm staying in isn't far from here," Cat replied. "I'm starving and I have an entire cold pizza that I'm eager to get to. You are welcome to join me…"

"An entire cold pizza?"

She laughed. "Yeah, I know it's hardly a culinary delight…"

"No! Actually, I was thinking that that sounds really good. How far are we going though? Can I carry my board there?"

"Yes, it's just up here," Cat said as she pointed along the beach.

Tom climbed down and helped her do the same.

"Wait, I need to change first," he said, already pulling down the zip of his wetsuit and lowering the top half of it.

"Um," he heard her say as he watched her eyes fall to his now bare chest. "I'm … going to … wait here … and face this way while you do that."

Tom saw her present her back to him, making

him laugh softly.

"I'll be right back. I have clothes over this way."

Cat stood still, the image of his chest still fresh in her mind. He was an attractive man, and he was waking her body up.

Tom quickly dumped his wetsuit, towel-dried his body and put on his cargo shorts and t-shirt. Following her up through the sand dunes, he was led into the back yard of a small house on the edge of them.

They climbed up the back steps onto a large deck spanning the length of the frontage that faced the water. Tom turned and looked out as he placed his surfboard down.

"Wow!" he exclaimed. "You get to stay here?"

"Yeah, I know," Cat said. "I'm really lucky. It's a great place to go to sleep and wake up. Hearing the waves is nice … soothing."

He heard her unlock the door and followed her inside. In the kitchen, he watched as she pulled a pizza box from the refrigerator.

"Gourmet meal is served," she said, looking happier than she had done since the moment he'd met her. "Come with me. Let's eat out on the back deck."

"Anywhere I can see and hear the sea, works for me."

They settled on the small outdoor sofa on the deck with the pizza box between them.

"Tessa said you were a nerd in high school," Tom said as he began to eat. "I find that kind of hard to believe."

Cat laughed. "Why?"

"Because you're so beautiful. I just can't get my head around the nerd thing."

She looked at him, once again blushing. "Thank you," she said. "That is a really lovely thing to say but believe me, I definitely was the nerd. And with my braces and freckles, half-inch thick glasses and a weird fashion sense, I definitely was your stereo*typical* nerd."

"You wore glasses?" Tom asked. "But you don't now…"

"No, I wear contacts now, most of the time," Cat replied. "But sometimes I prefer to have a break and wear glasses."

"You've probably got that sexy secretary thing going on when you have your glasses on," Tom said. In response, he saw her laugh again. It was such a great sound that he felt he could always listen to it. Always.

"Once again I have no idea how to respond to that," she replied, grinning.

Tom saw her grab a slice of pizza. He watched as she took a bite. The focus on her lips was unavoidable. They were very kissable lips, and watching her eating pizza was making him slightly turned on. He quickly moved his eyes to the pizza box and took a slice out for himself. Leaning back, he purposely turned his sight to the ocean.

"This is nice. Thank you for joining me. Sometimes life feels so lonely for me," she said, looking at his profile side on.

He turned to her and nodded in agreement. "For me, too. Sometimes it feels like no matter how many people are around me, I still feel alone."

"You're really easy to talk to," she said, giving him a warm feeling inside. "I'm kind of glad that I walked into the café with my dress wet and see-through."

"Oh, me too. That is a moment I don't think I'll ever forget," he replied, and they both laughed.

Soon the pizza was gone and the feeling of sunset approaching encroached.

"I need to get going, but thank you, Cat. I have very much enjoyed your company today - and your cold pizza," Tom said. "I hope you will want to come and see me on the beach tomorrow?"

Cat nodded. She didn't usually put trust in people so easily or so quickly, but she felt safe with him.

"I'd really like that. What time?"

"Let's go for 10 o'clock. The tide should be good then. Does that suit you?" he asked and she nodded. "Okay. Keep safe, Cat, and I hope to see you tomorrow."

Cat watched as he made his way down the steps and back along the beach. For a long while, she had been able to forget her stresses and her fears. Now they kicked in again as she made her way indoors, making sure to double-lock the door behind her.

Inside, as she prepared for a quiet evening alone in front of the television, she pulled out her mobile phone. She'd neglected it for most of the day. The notification that she had ten text messages waiting quickly turned her mood from happy to full of dread.

'You can't leave me. I love you.'
'Where are you?'
'Why have you run? You're my girl.'
'I'm coming to find you.'

Cat shut the phone off and tossed it aside. For whatever reason, technology had failed her and blocking Tony's number hadn't worked. All he did was go and buy another SIM card. What she really needed to do was get a new number. She would do that the next day. It was a hassle to have to do it but she didn't want every day to continue to be filled with stress whenever she looked at her phone. Especially days like she'd just had. She knew not to read anything into Tom's friendly outlook toward her but it did feel good to have someone to talk to and relax with. And it certainly didn't hurt to have that person look as good as he did. Dark hair, dark eyes and very kissable lips. Yes, he certainly fell under that classic term, 'tall, dark and handsome'.

CHAPTER 4

Tom woke the next morning with full memory of the lips that had tempted him the day before. He hadn't kissed her. He hadn't even really flirted with her. But he most definitely had been *affected* by her. It would be nice to be close to someone again - physically close. He hadn't even really delved into that area of life yet. At eighteen, when he'd made that stupid mistake, he had already lost his virginity to a girl from his school, but that had been an awkward three or four times only. Neither of them had meant anything to each other. They were just two teenagers, keen to get on and just 'do it'. Now he looked forward to learning those skills properly with someone he could give his love to and someone who could love him in return.

Jumping out of bed and going into the bathroom, he heard his father downstairs. Tom and his father didn't get along. They never had before Tom had gone to prison and after a while, his father had stopped visiting him there. It was as if he'd decided to just forget about his son. Since Tom had been released and come home, he'd only seen his father a handful of times. For that he was glad.

Quickly he showered and dressed, and then prepared himself for seeing his father again.

"Dad," he said simply.

His father turned and gave Tom an unwelcome look. He didn't even try to hide his disappointment in his son.

"I'm packing and then heading off to Los Angeles. One of my second cousins on my father's side has passed away so I'll be staying for a month or so."

"To do what?" Tom dared to ask.

He saw his father move closer. He was intimidating, even to Tom after ten years of dealing with extreme men in prison.

"To do whatever the hell I want," his father said with a menacing tone in his voice. "Tell your mother I'll see her when I see her."

In disbelief, Tom watched as his father went into the room he occupied by himself, then came out with a suitcase and just walked out. To Tom, that was the relationship from hell. Why his mother had put up with it for so long was beyond understanding to Tom. He knew deep in his heart that he was absolutely *never* going to treat a woman like his father treated his mother. Never. *Ever*.

~ ~ ~

"Hey," he heard the sensual voice say from

behind him just as he'd changed into his wetsuit on the sand.

Turning around he saw Cat dressed in a plain black one-piece swimsuit and a sarong wrapped around her hips. Her hair seemed to be tied back in a plait. Tom couldn't stop his eyes falling to her chest and remembering how she'd looked in that dress…

Raising his eyes quickly once he realized what he'd done, he saw that she'd seen him. Both of them laughed.

"Good morning, Cat," he said, chuckling and blushing at the same time. "Were you watching me change into my wetsuit?" he asked, the grin on his face growing larger.

Now it was her turn to blush. "Well it only seemed fair, given how much of me you've already seen," she quipped back, making him nod with a smirk of humor on his face.

"Touché!" he said, enjoying how happy she seemed now compared to the day he'd first met her. "And did you enjoy the view as much as I did?"

She laughed more but still nodded. "Oh, yeah."

Flirting was new to Cat but she found she was enjoying it with him. It was light-hearted and she truly believed that he read nothing into it. There was no danger in it with him. It was just fun.

"Hmm! Well, Miss Pervy, are you ready to go

out there?" he asked, inclining his head toward the ocean.

Cat felt nervous but excited also. "I think so, but we won't go out too far, right?"

"You'll be safe," Tom replied. "We'll stay as close in as we can, just to get you used to being on the board. Don't worry, you won't be riding any waves today. Just sitting and paddling is a good place to start."

She nodded. "Okay."

"First, you need to put this on," Tom said as he grabbed the spare wetsuit. "I'll need to adjust it to get it to fit as best I can get it."

Cat accepted the suit, undid her sarong and placed it on the sand, and then endeavored to put the wetsuit on. Not having worn one before, it turned out to be a bit more challenging than she'd imagined. When she had finally gotten her legs into the bottom half, she looked up and saw Tom standing with his arms crossed, seeming to enjoy the show immensely.

She laughed. "It's not as easy as you made it look, is it?"

He smiled at her and came forward. "I can help you if you want…"

Looking into his eyes as he stood so close, she wondered if she couldn't be tempted to forego the surf lesson altogether and just take him back to the house.

Such thoughts needed to be discarded. "Yes, please," she said meekly.

Tom moved around her and helped her to put her arms in and bring the wetsuit fully up. As she felt him gently lift her hair up and out of the way in preparation for pulling up the zip at the back, his fingers lightly swept over her neck and shoulder. It was the first physical contact she'd had with anyone in months. It was also right on an erotic spot of her body. Not thinking to stop herself, she moved her head slightly to the left and when his fingers found their way back there, she moaned.

Tom saw her reaction to his simple act of moving her hair out of the way so he could just zip the back of wetsuit up. When he saw her head move he wasn't sure if he was imagining her reaction or not, so moved his fingers back to the same spot. When she moaned, he felt his body instantly jump to life. He looked at where his fingers were. He wanted to lean forward and kiss her there, to see if she would like it. In truth, he felt pretty sure that she *would* like it, but was he allowed to? He hadn't yet gained confidence in making love with a woman. His teenage sexual experience wasn't real. It wasn't as it was meant to be. Even as a teenager he had known that.

"Cat?" he asked, determined to be sure if he was misreading her body signs.

"Hmm?" he heard her express with a question in her tone.

He looked at her. She wasn't moving away from his touch. She wasn't moving away at all.

"Can I kiss you here?" he asked boldly, his voice low and husky again.

She heard the change in his voice and it was like an electric shock moving straight to her core. Her body was pulsating in arousal. She wanted to stay in that moment and not move from it at all.

"Yes," she said, almost in a whisper. "Please."

Tom caressed the same small spot for a little longer with his fingertips and then leaned in and placed his lips where his fingers had just been. That close to her skin, he could smell a scent, perhaps a body lotion or some kind of soap. Combined with the smell of the sea air, it was intoxicating to him. He let his lips caress the tiny spot. When he moved to pull away, he heard her quiet voice call out to him.

"Don't stop."

He kissed her there again and became aware that her body was beginning to lean backward slightly toward him. Afraid that she would lean back too closely and feel how hard he was, he moved as she did, trying to keep the distance between them steadily apart.

"Why are you moving away from me?" she asked, surprising him with her candidness.

"Because I don't want…"

"Press against my back," he heard her say and now he moaned. She was going to drive him crazy. He could see it already.

Slowly he eased his body forward until his chest touched her back. His hands rose up and he started to lightly stroke her arms. She wouldn't be able to truly feel the impact of it through the thick wetsuit, but it felt like a natural thing for him to do. He kissed her neck further and she moved so that the gap he'd tried to maintain between their hips, was now closed.

Cat felt him pressing against her and loved what she could feel. Even through the two sets of wetsuits, it was evident to her.

"You are turned on, too," she said.

"Yes. Very," he replied, in between kisses.

She turned around then and met his lips with hers. After the initial surprise, Tom relaxed and let his lips enjoy the feeling of hers on his. He felt 28 and 18 all at the same time, like he was mature but he was immature. Experienced and inexperienced. Her tongue pushed into his mouth and he kissed her back passionately, slipping his arms around her and holding her as close to him as he could. He could feel her moving her hips against his and was glad they had so much material between them.

They stood like that for a long time, arms

wrapped around each other whilst their lips and tongues caressed and danced. When they heard voices in the distance they pulled apart.

"Wow," he said, making her laugh. "I … wow."

Cat felt aroused and happy … and free.

"But I did promise to get you out there, so now, please. I need to zip you up," he said. Once she'd turned around he quickly zipped the back of the wetsuit up and moved away from her. "Grab that board."

He watched as she tried to maneuver the board from the sand and carry it. It did seem funnily large compared to her, making him chuckle quietly.

"It will be easier to carry if you try this way," he said and showed her how to manage it better. "Okay, let's go."

For the next two hours, Cat was introduced to the joy of moving through the water while lying on the board. At times they stopped out past the small waves, sat up facing one another, and just talked. The combination of the feel and sound of the water, the freshness of the air she was breathing, and the enjoyment she was getting from his company, gave her hope that she *could* have a new life. It *was* possible.

"The tide's changing. We need to go back to shore," he called out and together they made their way back to the sturdiness of the sand. "How did you find that?" he asked once they were on solid ground again.

Cat felt invigorated and her smile said as much.

"Oh my god, that was amazing! Can we do that again another day?"

He smiled at her. "We can. Tomorrow I go back to work for another five days, but then I'll have a couple of days off."

A frown appeared on her face. Would she still be around for another week? Or would she be found and be driven to move on again?

"What?" Tom asked, wondering what had caused her to look so serious all of a sudden.

"I don't know if I'll still be here next week, Tom."

The words hit him hard. It made no sense that they did. He'd only just met her but they *did* affect him. He said nothing for a few minutes while they moved the boards up the beach and then stripped off their wetsuits. They'd never done it together before today but they seemed perfectly in tune as she turned around and let him unzip her, and then they reversed. As they used towels to dry off a bit he fought to keep his mind off her body. Especially when she leaned forward to dry off the front of her legs. Then he *definitely* had to look away and think about how the clouds were looking.

"Those clouds are looking ominous. It's going

to pour down any minute," he said, once he actually focused on what he'd only been pretending to look at.

"Do you want to come to the house with me?" Cat asked. "I can whisk us up something to eat."

Tom nodded. If there was a chance he only had today with her, he had no plans to waste it.

They walked in silence to the house and up the back steps. Just as they entered the back door, they heard heavy drops start. At first, they were spaced apart but then quickly began absolutely pouring down, sounding more like hail on the back porch than rain. Cat closed the back door and they moved to the kitchen. Through the small windows over the sink, they could both see the level of downpour that was happening. It was a soothing sound, like a heartbeat on the roof and windows.

Tom watched as she moved around the kitchen, looking in cupboards and the refrigerator. Finally, she held up a carton of eggs in one hand and mushrooms in the other.

"Mushroom omelet?" she asked and saw him nod.

"I'm good at making omelets if you want me to make them," he said and saw her smile softly at him.

"I am sure you are," Cat said, grinning at him. "But today *I* cook."

He watched her as she fluttered about. His eyes were focused on her but his mind was focused on the words she'd said to him earlier. He needed an explanation of what she meant but he would wait until she was finished cooking. She was still wearing only a bathing suit and the sarong around her hips so it was no difficulty just watching her. He was glad she was a one-piece girl. No matter how much guys had always expressed enthusiasm for women in bikinis, he really did find one-piece suits far more appealing. Something about there being so little on show was preferable to him than being able to see almost everything, like some bikinis were like. He could still clearly see the outline of her breasts. She had a figure that some would call curvy, some would call heavy, some would probably even venture to call overweight. He thought she was perfect. He wouldn't have enjoyed looking at her half as much if she was skinny. No, she had a body he liked. A *lot*.

Aware he was causing his body to be too awake again, he sighed and looked out the window.

"What was that sigh for?" he heard her ask, amusement in her voice.

She watched as his head turned to face her again. He opted whether to be honest or polite. He went with honest.

"I was trying to control my arousal," he said with such stark frankness that she looked stunned before they both burst out laughing.

"Okay, well, that is yet another statement from you that I have absolutely no response to," she said, chuckling still. "But the omelets are ready so here you go. We can either sit here at the table or on the sofa in the lounge. Your choice."

"I'm definitely more a sofa man," Tom replied.

Cat smiled and nodded. Tom followed as she led him into the living room. The two of them sat close on the sofa and began eating.

"Hmm, this is really good. *Almost* as good as mine," he said, teasing her. He still hadn't forgotten what she'd said on the beach. "So why might you not be here next week?"

Cat looked at him. She liked his eyes. They were easy to look into.

"Last night, after you left, I had a heap of text messages on my phone from my ex. He didn't sound like he had any idea where I was but I know it's just a matter of time," she said.

"Surely he'll just give up, won't he?" Tom asked. "You haven't messaged him back, have you?"

"No," Cat said as she shook her head. "First thing this morning I called my phone company and got a new number so I won't receive any more messages from him. But now I wonder if I did the right thing. If I'd let the messages continue to come through, I might have a better knowledge of where his head is at and what he's doing. Now I feel like he could be creeping up on me and I'd never know."

Tom was both shocked and angry at what she was saying.

"Well, you said he doesn't know about the friend that owns this place, right?" he asked and saw her nod. "Then stay here. It might be the safest place you can be. Stay here and stay inside. Keep away from shops and everything. I am happy to pick up anything you need from the supermarket or whatever."

"Thank you, Tom, but how can I live like that? It would be like being in a prison."

He wanted to shout at her 'it would not be anything like being in a prison' but held back just in time. It was a near-miss of telling her about his past, and he didn't want to do that. Not yet anyway. The moment he said he'd killed someone, what would happen? Would she call the police and tell them he was harassing her? The possible flow-on effect from telling anyone he'd been in jail was a constant fear inside of him.

Refocusing on their conversation instead of his own personal concerns, he looked at her. "It might not be enjoyable but it would only be for a while. I mean, how long will he pursue you? You said he has other women to keep him company. Surely they won't put up with him chasing *you* all the time. Not for very long anyway."

Cat sat quietly. She was happy to think that she was being paranoid. She would rather she *was* paranoid. She nodded and quietly finished the rest of her meal. When she'd put her plate down on the coffee table in front of them, she sat back and let her head rest on the back of the sofa.

Tom watched her. He thought he could probably sit and watch her all day and all night and never get tired of it. She had closed her eyes as he finished his meal and put his plate next to hers. When he looked back at her, he saw she had opened her eyes again and was looking at him.

"If I were leaving next week, what would you like to happen between us now?" she asked. He was in awe of her for having the guts to ask questions so straightforwardly.

"How do you do that?"

"What?"

"You ask questions that other people would want the answer to but would be too embarrassed or worried about to ask. How do you have the courage to ask so directly?"

She smiled at him. "I don't know. I think that my belief that life is short, makes me also believe that if I want to do things in my life, I have to get on and do them. There won't always be a tomorrow and part of that is also asking the questions that I want answers to. I don't want to end my life with a long series of 'what ifs' glaring in front of me. I want to proactively do - and ask - what I want to before it's too late."

Tom had nothing to say to that. She was incredible. She was beautiful. Everything about her was amazing to him. He couldn't do anything else at that moment except pull her to him and kiss her. Deeply. Passionately. Just in case she needed to know how he felt about her, he needed to make sure she knew.

Cat let herself sink against him. She hadn't thought she'd missed physical intimacy but she knew now that she had. She wanted him. She needed him. Her body was screaming out to be closer to him. Much, *much* closer.

Lips and tongues caressing, Tom found himself nudged back so that he was lying down on the sofa with Cat on top of him.

Straddling him, her lips never left his, like they were working together in perfect harmony. It seemed a long time since she'd been intimate with a man.

For Tom, it really was a long time since he'd touched a woman. It had been ten years since he'd been sexual, and even the sex he'd had back then wasn't fulfilling in any way other than the 'let's just do it' way it was intended to be as a horny teenager. He still felt like a horny teenager, but he didn't want to act like one.

Cat felt his hands in her hair, holding it and using it to pull her even closer to him. It was as if he wanted to hold her as tightly as he could, and not let her go. The feeling drove her on in her hunger and started to rub her hips against his.

The movement was deliciously unbearable to Tom, like sweet with sour, or fire with ice. He knew he was as hard as he possibly had ever been with the intense feeling of being turned on that he was experiencing. Cat rubbing against him was driving his arousal on even further. He made no move for anything else. Her lips, her tongue and her hips were all moving in unison that was far too enjoyable for him to stop or change anything.

Cat felt like she was swimming in a warm, deep pool. Her mind was turned off to any thoughts as she focused on all the muscles throughout her body, feeling like someone was lightly plucking them. Her heart was beating heavily. She could feel her pulse in different parts of her body, but the pulsating in her core felt like it was booming. Being stimulated by the feeling of his hardness underneath her, she was happy indulging in rubbing herself against it. The way they were moving together was beautiful. She hardly knew the guy underneath her, but it was absolutely *beautiful.*

After a long while, Tom heard her moaning heavily. The sound was like an orchestral harmony to him. He knew she had things that she worried about but he suspected that right at that moment she was finally free of worrying about them. The sounds she was making drove him on too.

All of a sudden she pulled herself upward slightly. She moved just enough to start sliding down the straps of her swimsuit. When the first strap almost reached her elbow, Tom reached up and stopped it from traveling any further.

"Cat," he said as he slid the strap back into place.

She waited for him to say more but that was all he said. She was left floundering. He didn't want her to undress. What did that mean? She pulled off him and sat back on the sofa, bewildered.

"You don't want me? You don't find me attractive?" she asked.

Tom sat up, wary of how any set of words he spoke at that moment could make her feel good or feel bad.

"I don't think you really need to ask that," he replied. "You know you are driving me crazy with how much you're turning me on. You are beautiful and sexy, and I know that you could feel what you do to me!"

Cat smiled. He was right. A part of her - the part that always felt ugly during high school years - wanted to feel rejected because of what she looked like. It made no sense and yet it made perfect sense. But he was right. She knew she turned him on just as much as he turned her on.

"Okay," she said. "Do we need to talk about why? *Why* you don't want to see me naked?"

Tom laughed softly, groaning at the same time. "Did you really just ask me that?" he asked her and she laughed in response. "You think I don't want to see you naked??"

"Well, you just stopped me from doing this," she said and started to slide one strap of her bathing suit down again.

Once more Tom reached up and firmly slipped the strap back up onto her shoulder as he laughed in an obviously teasing tone.

"Don't do that!" he said in mock sternness.

"Okay, Tom," Cat replied. "But give me a reason why. Please."

He was silent for a long while as he lightly caressed her cheek with his fingers.

"There are things about me that you don't know."

"And there are things about me that *you* don't know," she replied. "That doesn't have to stop us from enjoying time together. Does it?"

"My things aren't little things," Tom said. "And I would rather you know me - *all* of me - before we cross that line."

"You don't like the just-sex thing, do you," she

said and saw him shake his head.

"No, I don't really have any desire for the just-sex thing. I'm here like this with you because I really, really like you," he said. "I think you are beautiful and funny, and sexy as hell. But I don't want you to give yourself to me like that until I am sure you know exactly who you are giving yourself to."

"Then tell me," she said, now serious and almost pleading. "Share with me who you are and what you've done that you think will make me turn away from you."

He sat up and positioned himself so that they were facing one another and he could hold her hand.

"Alright. When I was 18 I went to a friend's place for a party. It was to celebrate finishing high school. It was an okay night but then these guys turned up. They were older than us and they were drunk or high or something. I don't know but they forced their way inside and started making trouble. They kept harassing the girls and shoving the guys. It was just really messy. We all got into a bit of a shoving and punching match but I punched a guy and he went down. Then he didn't move. I punched him once, Cat, and that was it."

"That was *it?*" she asked, confused.

Tom nodded, his face incredibly sad with tears emerging. "He was dead. I punched a guy and he fell to the ground right in front of me … dead."

He watched her face as she processed what he'd said. He saw confusion first, as if she couldn't comprehend what he was saying. Her face changed to that of horror as she finally did comprehend. He sat silent, wondering if she would speak.

"You killed someone?" she asked and he nodded, the tears now flowing. Still, ten years on, he could visualize the guy lying on the floor, still … so very, very still. "And what happened?"

"I went to prison. For manslaughter," he explained as he wiped his eyes. Usually, he could keep his tears to a minimum but they weren't so easily controlled this day it seemed.

"For how long?" Cat asked.

"I was away for ten years. I got out just a few months ago," Tom answered.

Cat let the story mull in her mind. The guy beside her - a gorgeous sexy guy who turned her on like no other guy ever had - had killed someone. That was big. That was scary. But the only question she really needed to ask was whether she felt safe with him and whether she thought he could hurt her.

"Did you think you would kill him when you punched him?" she asked.

"No! Of course not!" Tom exclaimed. "He was a jerk but he was only a few years older than me.

No matter how much of an asshole he was, he didn't deserve to die!"

"But … that must have been horrible for you. Even putting aside the fact that you went to jail. How have you dealt with having taken someone's life?"

He looked at her. No-one else had ever asked him that. Not one person before her had asked him how he felt about having killed that guy. In doing so, she was highlighting to him again how much he loved her straightforwardness and commitment to asking questions straight out. It was refreshing.

The tears flowed more fluidly, as he tried to put into words how he felt.

"I … I have to live with that knowledge for the rest of my life. I took a mother and father's son from them. I took a brother from a young girl and two young boys. I took a friend from a load of people. I took away his right to live a long life. *I* did that. That is all on *me*. No-one else. And there hasn't been a day when I haven't thought about that," he said. "But this week, with you, I have thought about it less. I like being with you. I feel okay when I'm with you, like I'm not some freak. But that was before I told you who I am…"

Cat understood what he was asking, without actually asking it. He wanted to know if she'd still want to know him after what she'd just learned.

She looked at him for a long time, saying nothing. Over and over in her head, she imagined the scene of the incident. A room full of teenagers. Older boys under the influence, invading and causing havoc. One guy throwing one punch. One guy down. Dead. If that wasn't a needless death, what was? But was anyone really to blame? Of course, he'd thrown the punch that killed the guy. But who would expect one punch to kill instantly? What are the chances of that even happening?

"Tom, you are never going to be able to bring that boy back," she started to say, stunning him. As if she weren't unique enough already, that line had never been thrown at him as an opening to how someone felt about him. "You were sentenced and you served the length of time that the justice system decided you had to, to pay for the crime you committed. It might always be with you that you killed him, but that doesn't mean that you shouldn't let yourself live. I get that you are starting over. You're fresh out of prison. You've got your job now and you have your surfing. But you are still placing too much emphasis on it. I'm not saying forget it happened but I have met you and I don't perceive you to be a violent person…"

"I'm *not!*" Tom cried out.

"I know," Cat said, smiling sadly. "I can tell that. So perhaps it isn't me who has to accept you despite what you have done. Perhaps it's *you.*"

He looked at her for a long while, wondering what she was saying. "I don't understand."

"When we walked in here earlier, I walked in with a man who has made me laugh and really feel more over the past couple of days than I have in ages. I walked in with a man who is sexy and I very much want to get naked. He is the man I walked in with," she said and cupped his face in her hands as she forced him to look right into her eyes. "And he is *still* the man who is sitting beside me. You haven't changed because of what you just told me. You are still *you*. And I still *want* you."

She leaned in and kissed him and Tom let her. He felt overwhelmed in emotion. The response wasn't anything like he would have expected. When she pulled away and looked at him, he was confused. Her reaction appeared to have stunned him.

Cat looked closely at him. She wasn't oblivious to the fact that she was sitting alone in a house with a man who had killed someone but she had to trust her ability to read people. He wasn't a bad guy. He was one of the *good* ones. If she was wrong in that assumption, then she might have already been in trouble the first moment she had let him into the house. No, he was a good one. She just needed to let him know that.

He watched as she stood and held out her hand

to him. Slowly he rose and took it, and found himself led into her bedroom. Once in there, she stood by the bed and took both of his hands in hers. He was still too shocked to be able to move.

Knowing he seemed fearful of pushing himself on her when she might not want it, Cat took matters into her own hands and reached up and kissed him. She moved her arms around him, caressing his lips with hers while moving her tongue into his mouth to find his. Eventually, she felt him warm up and his arms move around her, pulling her hard against him. They stood like that for a long while, letting their passion build again until she could bear it no longer.

"It's coming off now, whether you like it or not," she said before pushing down the straps of her bathing suit.

"Oh, I like it," he said, making her laugh as she removed her sarong and her bathing suit completely. Before him stood a beautiful, naked woman. His breath deepened as he simply stood and looked.

"Okay, you need to look less, and undress more," Cat said, humor in her tone.

When her words actually sunk in, Tom laughed with her and quickly removed his t-shirt, shorts and underwear. He felt like he was right back there - eighteen again. A teenager keen to get on with it, but having absolutely no idea what he was supposed to do.

"I don't want to rush," he said, unintentionally voicing his thoughts. "Please."

Cat moved into his arms and kissed him again, loving the first feeling of their two naked bodies pressed up against one another.

Tom watched her pull away and move onto the bed, lying down on her side and inviting him to do the same. As he moved onto the bed, he was astounded by her body. He wanted to explore it. Instead of lying down as she was, he knelt beside her. Reaching down and kissing her lips softly, he let his hands begin a journey. At first, he was shy so avoided all her private parts, letting his hands move softly and slowly up and down her arm and then her hip.

"Move onto your tummy," he said and watched as she did so. That was better. Now he could run his hands together over her entire back and down, caressing her buttocks and moving to her thighs. It didn't escape his attention that as he moved his hands around the area, her legs parted slightly, but he wasn't ready to go there yet. He still knew so little about a woman's anatomy. His rushed sexual encounters in his teen years hadn't comprised of investigating that area closely … not with his hands anyway.

His hands continued down her legs, caressing and touching her everywhere, right down to her ankles, before moving back again. When he came back up he indulged in massaging her upper back and her shoulders. Aware now of the spot that had affected her so much earlier that day, he kissed where he had then. Instantly he heard her moan out a soft sound of appreciation. He spent time there, not wanting to rush anywhere else.

"Cat," he said quietly, needing to tell her.

"Yes?"

"I don't know…" he started to say and then felt stupid. He was a 28-year-old man. How could he not know…

Under his hands, she turned over and pulled him down to kiss her. He lay down, alongside the length of her.

"You don't know what?" she asked gently, her face still close to his.

"I went inside when I was 18. I don't know … how to … make you feel good."

She smiled at him. "You are already making me feel good, Tom."

With her comment, he was happy but frustrated at the same time, and she saw it. He felt her hand guide his downward, introducing one of his fingers to her clitoris. As she did, she used words to talk to him and even in that, he was thankful that she was such a straightforward talker. She had no embarrassment or uneasiness about her as she guided and moved his hand against her. She also had no hesitation in asking him to move down and explore with his lips and his tongue.

Although embarrassed to be receiving tuition of sorts, Tom was very happily intrigued by her body and learning how to please her.

Cat, in turn, was very pleased with his first effort of exploration, as her body convulsed against his tongue. As far as a student went, she was pretty sure he'd earn an A+ for effort and success.

When he moved back up her body, she had a condom ready. Tom knelt still as she slipped it over him. This part, he knew he could do. He lay between her thighs and kissed her, letting their desire for one another build to the levels it had been earlier before he slid forward and found himself engulfed by her warmth.

"Ohh," she heard him groan out heavily as he pushed as far into her as he could go. He lay still for a moment, just concentrating on how it felt. When he opened his eyes and looked into hers he liked what he saw.

"You feel good," she said, her eyes full of desire.

Tom nodded and kissed her again. Slowly he began moving. He didn't want it to be over too soon. Always before, when he was a teenager, it had been a rush to get to the finish line. He didn't want that now. Now he wanted to really *feel* it. He also wanted to see, feel and hear how she was feeling. He pulled away from the kiss and watched her face as he very slowly moved in and out of her. Now and then she would open her eyes, look at him, and reach for him to kiss her. In between those moments, her eyes were closed and her mouth showed how incredibly aroused she was. Tom thought he could stay right where he was forever or, if not forever, definitely for hours.

Cat reveled in the feelings that came from him moving as slowly as he was. It was nice, his determination to not rush. She could feel herself being stimulated and even though she'd only had an orgasm not long before, the slow and steady rubbing of his pelvis against her clitoris resulted in her reaching that point again. She was overwhelmed. That had never happened before when a man was inside of her. After recovering from that, she was eager to hear him reach that point. She was caught in what she should do. She wanted him to extend it out if he really wanted to. She also wanted to hear and feel him reach that blissful place.

She needn't have considered the option of either lying still or moving her hips to help him along. Soon after her orgasm, he started to naturally move slightly faster and she could tell he was on his way. He was on his own journey of pleasure. Knowing that moving her hips could result in him reaching climax earlier than he wanted to, Cat lay perfectly still. It wasn't her usual way but she felt that for him, this time at least, he deserved to take it at his own pace. As quickly or slowly as he wanted. When he was moving quicker, she was rid of all thoughts as the feelings that flowed through her body were incredible. He felt amazing, moving into her as fast and as hard as he was. Now and then he would kiss her deeply. It was astonishing, just how good it felt. It was like they fitted together perfectly … like they had been made for each other.

Finally, she felt and heard him climax. His body convulsed heavily and even she could feel it pounding through him. The power of his release was overwhelming enough to her. She could hardly imagine how it had felt to him. After a long while of being slumped on top of her, he finally lifted his head and grinned at her.

"Sorry, I'm probably squashing you," he said, making her laugh softly.

"No, it feels nice having you right where you are."

"Hmm," he said quietly. He kissed her lips gently, then with more hunger. "Oh, I should get rid of this," he said, pulling out to release the latex gripping him. The withdrawal left Cat feeling empty all of a sudden. She actually felt regret that he had moved out of her. That was a first for her.

"Will you stay with me?" she asked him when he came back to the bed, stretched out and pulled her into his arms.

"For the night, do you mean?"

She giggled slightly. "Yes," she said. "All night. Like a sleepover."

He moved slightly so he could look into her eyes.

"I would like that … a lot! I know this is going to sound weird, coming from a 28-year-old man, but I need to go home to my mother." He laughed softly, knowing it sounded ridiculous. "Sorry but she is alone there and since I got out she has been non-stop worried that I'm going to do something to get myself put back into jail." He paused for a moment before he spoke again. "Cat, I just wouldn't feel good staying out all night tonight."

She nodded. "I understand."

Tom could sense her disappointment. "But you could come and stay with me, I suppose."

"Stay in the same house as your mother?" Cat asked, bursting out laughing. "I don't think I could … we could… "

Suddenly she was giggling at the thought and he laughed with her.

"Don't you have a father?" she asked when their laughter died down. Immediately she felt Tom's body tighten. "You have mentioned your mother but not a father."

"My father isn't much of a father, and he's even less of a husband. For as long as I can remember, he's only passed through home now and then. I don't even remember him ever acknowledging Mom when he's seen her. It's odd because when I've met people who knew him when he was younger, they've all raved about what a great man he is - a 'great member of the great Santini family'. He doesn't show that side to us. Never has. Probably never will."

"Santini. That's a nice name."

"Hmm. When I met Cameron from the States, he said there is a huge family of us there," Tom said. I didn't even know until then that I had relations in America. Most of them are firefighters apparently, all doing great things for the community."

"I think that is what your nature is, too. You would probably fit right in to a family like that," Cat said.

"Do you think?" Tom asked. "I don't know. I have so many things to work through."

He saw her raise her head and look at him before she spoke again. "I think you are a good man, Tom Santini. You have spent too long thinking otherwise, but you *are* a good man. I wouldn't be here with you if I didn't believe that."

Tom pulled her to him then and kissed her deeply. "Don't disappear, Cat. Please," he said quietly, almost a whisper. "This isn't just sex to me."

"I know. I knew that before I took my bathing suit off," she replied, smiling. "I can't promise anything, Tom, because I have to put my safety first, but I can certainly promise that I don't *want* to leave. I want to spend time with you and get to know you better. I want to learn about your family and what your life was like when you were growing up. There's just too much yet. I won't leave. If I do, you know it's because I've *had* to, not because I've wanted to."

Tom kissed her again and pulled her onto him as he rolled onto his back. This time he lay back and let her lead the way. Like that, he truly believed he was in heaven as he lay still and watched her, moving up and down on him. Yes, teenage sex was to be forgotten. This was much, much better…

~ ~ ~

"I need to go," he said, a long time later. "It won't always be like this, I promise. It's just that she's alone tonight and I haven't talked to her about you. Once I do that, I will feel better about staying with you."

Cat smiled at him. "It's fine," she said. "I get it. And you wanting to watch out for your Mom is sweet. It only makes me more sure of how good a man you are."

Tom kissed her gently and they walked together to the door. "Keep safe."

"Will you come and see me tomorrow after work?" she asked and saw him nod.

"I'd love that," Tom replied. "I'll be here around six if that's okay."

"Yeah, of course. I'll be here."

"I'll bring dinner," he said.

Cat smiled and kissed him before he walked out and she locked the door. Unknown to both of them, someone was in the dark, down the side of the house.

That person was *not* happy to see what he'd seen.

CHAPTER 5

Tom found his mother calm and not worried at all when he got home.

"Oh, someone's got a *girlfriend*," she said when he leaned in to kiss her on her forehead.

"How could you possibly…"

"A mother knows!" she said forcefully. Then added onto the end of that, in a humorous tone, "And you smell of her perfume."

He grinned at her. "Have you eaten? Do you want me to cook something?"

"Oh, I had some soup that I made today. There's some in the pot on the stove if you want some," she replied.

Tom moved to the kitchen and filled a large mug with the thick soup that smelled heavenly, before returning to sit near her.

"So, who is she and how has she captured your heart so quickly?" she asked and saw Tom smile.

"She is a lovely young woman and we've only recently met so I don't think hearts are involved yet."

"Your face says otherwise. If she makes you happy, just enjoy it because one day you can feel like you love someone deeply and the next day that person can just check out, like they just forget you're there. After that, all you have are memories of all the good times you had, and the feelings you once shared together."

It was the first time his mother had brought up anything about her relationship with his father - assuming she *was* talking about her and his father.

"Why do you stay married to him?" he blurted out, intending to think the words rather than verbalize them. He was pleased to hear his mother simply start talking about their marriage, not fazed at all by the question.

"I don't know really," she replied. "When you and your brother were young it was for the security of having a home and you having two parents. Then, when you went to jail, I didn't really care anymore how he treated me. And it has been easy living here. I never had to work, you know. Always, he's paid for the roof over our heads and the food in our bellies. I don't know why but he's always done it and he's never let me down that way."

"But you don't really get *him*, do you? Don't you want a companion by your side?"

"Hmph! At my age…"

"Mom, you're only 50 years old! That isn't too old to start over with someone who will enjoy actually spending time with you."

She smiled at him. He was a good kid, this one.

She'd always known it, despite what others had said about him over the years.

"You just make sure that *you* are happy. If you are, don't waste a second. Enjoy it while you can."

"I was thinking I might stay there … overnight … tomorrow night," he said, definitely now feeling like a teenager, asking for a forbidden sleepover.

His mother burst out laughing. "You aren't asking your mother for permission to sleep with your girlfriend, are you?"

He smiled at her sheepishly. "No, not exactly, but I know that you worry when I'm out at night…"

"Oh, thank you, Tom, but you are a grown man and I'm not worried about you now. I was when you first came home. I worried how difficult it would be for you to adjust to normal life again but I see you and I have watched you get yourself together. You've got a good job that you enjoy, and now you have a young lady to keep company. Don't worry about me. You already convinced me that I don't have to worry about you. Enjoy her. Life is too short; it really is. You have to make the most of every moment."

For a moment Tom felt slightly tearful, having listened to her speaking in such a way. He wanted to tell her to take her own advice and get out of the house to enjoy life again. Hearing her say that she believed in him was enough for now. It was a start.

"Go to her now, if you want to, Tom," his mother said. "I am fine. I'm a big girl now, you know!"

Tom laughed at her but sat with her while he finished his soup.

"Are you sure? I am happy to stay here with you."

"I know you are," she said. "No, really - go to her. You will have to come home in the morning to get ready for work, won't you?"

Tom nodded. It would be easier to take his stuff with him, but this way he could check on her in the morning.

"Alright," he said as he stood and took his bowl out to the kitchen to rinse. "I love you, Mom."

"I love you too, Tom."

~ ~ ~

Walking along the beach to the house Cat was staying in, Tom felt free and truly happy for the first time in over a decade. His life was truly coming together.

He hoped she wouldn't mind him just turning up like he was, having already told her he couldn't stay. Maybe he should turn and go home, and just see her tomorrow as planned.

After arguing with himself, he decided to walk forward. She could always ask him to leave and, knowing that she was a straight talker, he believed she *would* ask him to leave if she wanted him to. That made it easier to keep walking toward her place. If she didn't want him there, she'd let him know. Easy.

From the beach, he was about to head up the path to the back porch and deck when he heard voices inside. Angry voices. No, one angry voice and one terrified voice. The latter sounded more like it was whimpering.

Tom took a deep breath. He had to think before he acted. He wouldn't find himself in the same situation now as he had before. Whatever was going on, he couldn't just barge in there and punch the person who was yelling.

He decided to move closer and remain out of sight to hear what was happening. Seeing a gap under the deck, he quietly moved forward and settled himself under there. The night was still. Not even a breeze was around him. Perfect for listening in on other people's conversations. It wasn't right but if Cat was in danger, he at least wanted to know.

"Why do you keep chasing me, Tony? What do you *want* from me?" he could hear Cat yelling out into the night.

"I want you to come home! You are meant to be mine. I love you. That is why I've been searching for you. And now that I find you, you're with another *man?*"

"We aren't a couple anymore. You moved on, remember?!" Cat yelled "You have other women. Go home and be content with them. I am not one of your women anymore!"

"You are still my *wife*," Tom heard the guy call out, surprising him. He hadn't heard anything about marriage in all that Cat had told him.

"We're separated! We've been separated for over a year! The divorce papers are drawn up and waiting for you to sign…"

"I'll never sign them. You don't get to decide if or when our marriage is over!"

"Fine! Let's stay married forever if that's what you want. You won't be able to marry any of your other women if you're still married to me. You know that, right? No matter who you meet or how you feel about them, you won't be able to *marry* them, if you refuse to approve our divorce. Is that really what you want?"

"You are my wife and you need to come home … with me … now!"

"No!"

Tom heard the desperation in Cat's voice but he knew he had to be careful. If he got caught up in a domestic fight, even between a husband and a wife, there was too great a chance that he could be put back in prison if something went wrong. He knew all too well that something could *always* go desperately wrong! But listening to her voice, he couldn't just leave her there with that guy, even if he was her husband. It was at times like this that he wished his brother was nearby. Graham was someone tough who could stand up to a bully like that and deal with him without having to worry about consequences as much as Tom had to.

He knew he should do something, but what? He could run home and call the police. But tell them what? That a man and woman were arguing? They probably wouldn't do anything - not unless he hit her and there was evidence of it. Tom would prefer to not let that happen and, besides, he didn't even know the address of the house. He'd only walked in from the beach, through the back door. He had no idea what the house number was. He'd have to walk around the house to find out, and then if a neighbor saw him walking through someone's yard and they called the cops … the situation was causing a headache to come on.

Tom was still under the back deck when he heard and saw Cat run down the stairs and toward the beach. As he heard the next set of steps coming, Tom grabbed a length of timber that was sitting near him and swung it around, hitting Tony in the legs and making him stumble down the stairs. As he lay at the bottom and gripped his legs in pain, Tom ran after Cat, not looking back in determination to not let Tony see his face.

When he got to the beach he saw her ahead of him. "Cat!"

She heard him calling and thought it was Tom but didn't want to risk being mistaken. When the large rock she had sat on only the day before with Tom came into view, she ducked behind it and waited quietly.

Tom saw where she went so could see that she was freaked out and wasn't sure who was chasing her. He slowed right down and started to call out to her when a thud came down on his shoulder, knocking him to the ground.

"Don't think you can take what's mine," a voice said in a menacing tone.

Tom lay still and Cat had to stop herself from running to him once she realized what had happened and who had hit who. Instead, she crouched lower behind the large rock and moved into a gap that was formed underneath the back of it. Tony must know she was there somewhere but it was worth the risk to hide further just in case he didn't know precisely where. It was getting dark and she and Tom both knew the beach just that little bit better than Tony did. He would be more lost without any light.

"Come out, Cat. You're my wife and it's time to come home now," she each heard Tony say. He sounded close but not as close as he had done when he'd said what he had to Tom.

Cat held her breath as much as she could, fearful that even the sound of her exhaling would bring him to her side. But how had he even found her? Only one friend had known where she was, and that was the owner of the house. Surely they hadn't called him, had they? She trusted them and they had deceived her by siding with him when they knew how he treated her? If so, it was definitely time to find some new friends.

Listening, she could hear Tony's voice moving further away still, but she dared not move. She would stay there all night if need be. He had stamina. He had proven that by the lengths he was going to, to bring her home, even though they had been separated for so long.

Tom continued to lie still. He was fine, although his shoulder would hurt when he moved. He believed he was best to just listen. He knew exactly where Cat was and if Tony got close enough to possibly see her, Tom would move but not before. Right now he was only meters from her. He was close enough to jump up and surprise Tony if that was what it would take to keep her safe. It sounded like Tony was off to the far left and moving further away. Tom expected that he would come back this way. He would have to, even if only to get back to the house Cat was staying in. He probably had a car parked there, so he would need to go back that way even if he was going to give up his search. But when would that be? How long would this guy keep walking up and down a dark beach, looking for her, before he might consider she'd gotten away and was right now making her way along the road instead?

Cat and Tom both heard him coming back their way. Each held their breaths as he passed by. Tom braced himself for whatever Tony would do to him as he walked past him again. He was ready when the boot met his stomach, but he still didn't reveal that he was awake. Instead, he clenched his fists as hard as he could, concentrating the pain there as he hoped he wasn't going to be kicked any more.

~ ~ ~

Tony looked around and could see a bunch of people walking down a path to the sand. They were young people, he knew, but old enough to question why he was standing over a guy who was lying on the sand, unmoving. He couldn't have that so quickly made his way back to the house he'd found Cat in. Gullible Cat. Did she really think that people she regarded as friends, would help her stay away from him? Naïve she was, to think that. He had the support of everyone they had known as a couple. He'd made sure of that before she'd ever left. He was the nice guy. She was the loser. That was how he had set their marriage up, and how he liked it. What he didn't like was her thinking her life was her own, to do what she wanted with it. No, she had consented to be his on their wedding day. To obey. That was what she had agreed to. Well, she wasn't obeying now, and she hadn't for over a year. In his opinion, that wasn't good enough.

He glanced back at the beach one more time before he made his way up the path and into the house. She would come back. Where else could she go? And when she came back, he would show her just how tired he was getting of playing this game.

Down the beach, Tom heard the voices coming closer so sat up. He looked down the beach toward the house but Tony was nowhere to be seen. The pain in Tom's shoulder was intense, as was the residual pain in his gut from having a boot planted in it.

"Hey man, are you okay? We thought you were dead there for a minute," one of the young guys said, running up to him.

Tom smiled at him. "Thanks, but I'm okay. Thanks though."

He watched as the guy ran off to join his friends in their walk along the beach. When they were a little further away, and after checking the other direction once more, he called out to her.

"Cat, it's me, Tom. He's gone … at least for

now. Can you come out?"

Cat heard him and taunted herself for a while, telling herself it could be Tony, playing a trick on her. But she had to argue back with herself again, that she knew it was Tom. His voice was completely different.

She took a breath and climbed out, hoping she wasn't falling for some kind of trick. When she saw Tom, she ran to him.

"I don't think we should linger here. Come with me. We're going back to my place," he said.

Cat said nothing. Certainly, she had no desire to step foot in that other house again. Tony was there and the person who owned it had fed her to a wolf. She had little in it that was hers. Clothing was easily replaced, even if she had to buy the cheapest items from a second-hand store to be able to afford anything.

Tom led the walk, always looking around before taking a few more steps. Finally, they were near the yard of his home. He stopped and indicated to Cat to crouch down.

"What are we doing?" she asked, whispering.

"I just want to be absolutely sure he isn't following us," Tom said. "I don't want to lead him to the house where my mother is."

Cat felt guilty for bringing her trouble into his life. Tom sensed it but didn't want to speak in case Tony was nearby. He would reassure her later.

Right now, he needed to know that all of them were safe, including his mother inside.

They remained still and quiet for a long while until he believed they had escaped successfully and were safe.

"Are you okay going inside? It will probably entail meeting my mother," Tom eventually said.

Cat felt the stress flow out of her as she chuckled as quietly as she could. "I'm ready."

They walked quietly to and in the door to the home.

"Mom, it's just me," he called out, giving warning so she wouldn't be frightened when she wasn't expecting him home. When he walked into the living room he saw she was awake and looking at the doorway. "And a friend. I hope you don't mind but I'd like her to stay here tonight. Mom, this is Cat."

Cat entered the room, walked up to the older woman and held out her hand. Tom watched as his mother graciously accepted the handshake and smiled.

"You are the young lass making my son smile," she said.

Cat laughed. It was an enjoyable reprieve from the strain of the previous few hours.

"I hope so, although I expect he's quite a hit with the ladies so I can't be sure," she replied.

Tom saw his mother burst out laughing; a sight

he'd rarely seen in his life.

"Oh, I like this one. She has fire in her spirit! I was just about to go to bed though so I shall say goodnight to you both. It is nice to meet you Cat. I hope to see you around here a lot."

Tom and Cat watched her leave the room. Once alone, they sat on the sofa together to finally relax.

"Do you think we got here definitely without being seen?" Cat asked.

"I hope so. I'd like to stay up a bit longer though, maybe with these lights off, so we can just watch outside for a while. I think he went back to your place so hopefully he is just sitting there, waiting for you to go back," Tom said as he stood, walked to turn off all the lights, and then returned to the sofa.

"I'm not going back there."

"You didn't tell me you were married," Tom said quietly.

"I know. I'm sorry. I find it difficult to regard him as my husband now so it's second nature to call him my ex," she said and paused a long while before giving him a sad smile and speaking again. "See, you aren't the only one with a past you don't want to openly discuss."

They opened the curtains slightly and he smiled at her as he gently moved some stray hair out of her eye. "I understand completely."

"This has been an unbelievable day," Cat said.

Tom nodded. "That it certainly has! Learning to surf, being on the run and finally getting me naked. It's been rough for you, alright."

Cat giggled at him. "I said it was unbelievable. Not all *bad* though."

"Oh, you liked learning to surf then," he said, teasing her, making her giggle more.

"Yes, I did! Highlight of my day." She waited a moment and then smiled at him. "After getting you naked that is."

"Good reply."

They sat in silence for a while longer, until Tom knew he would have to go to sleep to get up early the following morning.

"I need to work tomorrow," he said.

"I know."

"You'll be safe here. Please do stay here."

"I'll be okay, Tom. I won't head out, I promise. He has really scared me tonight. Especially when he hit you…"

"I'm fine," Tom replied. "Come on, I'm taking you to bed."

"Oh! That seems a bit naughty in your mother's house."

"*You're* naughty. There will be none of that luscious nakedness tonight, Fair Cat."

"Fair Cat?!"

"Yes … well, okay, what about Fine Cat then?"

he said and she started giggling again. "Foxy Cat? Yes! Foxy Cat! Perfect! Come on, Foxy Cat," he said as he held out his hands and pulled her up from the sofa and into his arms. "I'm quite looking forward to being able to hold you all night."

They walked quietly upstairs and toward his bedroom. "The bathroom is there if you want to use it first," he said, pointing to a partially closed door.

Tom saw her nod and silently duck inside, closing the door behind her. Giving her space for a few minutes, he went into his room, switched on the light and quickly closed the curtains. He left the door open as he lay on his bed and let his mind replay the day. It was the craziest day in his life, he was sure. So much had happened but amongst the bad crazy was some really good crazy. That made him smile.

He heard the bathroom door open before Cat appeared in his doorway, looking shy and nervous. Quietly Tom stood up, stopped and kissed her softly on the lips, and then left the room to visit the bathroom himself.

While he was out of the room, Cat sat on the bed. At least it was a large one and not a tiny one he would have had as a kid. Although then she would have had to lie on top of him all night. She smiled at the ridiculous thought.

She undressed, glad that when Tony had arrived

at least she had gotten properly dressed in her sweat pants and hoodie. It would have been even more horrific if she'd had to run along the beach and into Tom's mother's home in her nightgown. These were her clothes now. They were all that she owned. She protectively folded them and put them on a chair in the room, along with her bra, which she'd slipped discretely off from underneath her t-shirt. By the time Tom returned to the room, she was relaxed in his bed.

After he entered and closed the door gently behind him, Tom whispered to her from across the room.

"I quite like this view," he said "You in my bed, I mean. Yes, indeed. I don't mind this at all."

Cat smiled and watched as he started to peel off his clothing, one layer at a time.

"Although next time I must time things the other way round so that it is me in the bed, watching *you* do a striptease," Tom continued.

Finally down to his boxers, he felt a little embarrassed that seeing her in his bed had played havoc with his body again. In boxers, there was just no hiding it, and she had definitely seen it.

"No naughtiness, remember!" she said with a sliver of a chuckle as he climbed into bed beside her.

"I promise to keep everything but my hands and lips off you," he replied as he blissfully gathered her into his arms. "This is a day of firsts for me. I've never slept beside anyone before."

She smiled at him and kissed him gently. "I'll be good. You won't even know I'm here."

Tom burst out laughing. "I don't think that's *ever* going to be possible."

They were silent as he turned off the light and she then cuddled into his chest and shoulder.

"What am I going to do, Tom?"

"I don't know," he replied. "But you need to keep safe, first and foremost. Maybe when I'm in town tomorrow, I can ask Toby for advice. I think he might know a lawyer or two, so maybe I can find out what your legal rights are," he said, wishing his brother was currently nearby and not in another country. "How long have you been separated?"

"Fourteen months."

"Okay. I can ask and see who can help anyway." He waited for a reply and when there was none, he continued. "Are you feeling alright about all this?"

He felt her once again cuddle into him, as if trying to get even closer to him, under his wing.

"I'll be better when this is over and I have my life back again completely. But for now - *right* now - I'm feeling pretty good. I am in bed with a gorgeous, hot-bodied man after all. What can I really complain about?"

She felt Tom smile and then kiss her forehead.

"Yeah, true. How about you turn over there and I can cuddle you while we fall asleep."

Cat turned and felt him move up behind her. He was still hard, and pressing against her, making her smile but seemingly not him.

"Um, maybe we can try it the other way around. I'm going to turn this way," Tom said as he removed from being pressed up so hard against her.

Cat laughed at him but happily turned over and huddled her chest against his back.

As she did, Tom became aware of her breasts pushing against him. He said nothing more but certainly thought to himself that it was going to be a long night.

CHAPTER 6

Waking up with a beautiful woman in his arms was something Tom had never experienced before. It had been late when he'd finally fallen asleep, being so aware that she was in bed with him, and him being so aroused. That feeling had seemed to take forever to go away.

Turning over and seeing her so close, already awake and looking at him, was something he didn't mind at all. Glancing at the clock he saw he'd woken a quarter-hour before his alarm was due to go off. Plenty of time to kiss and cuddle.

He moved in close to her and she eagerly welcomed him into her arms. Limbs wrapped around each other and he was hungry to have her.

"I may need to stop at the chemist today to be more prepared for waking up beside you," he said. "If you are going to keep staying here, that is."

Cat smiled at him and reached down to stroke him through his boxers. "I'd like to stay if I'm not imposing on you and your family."

"No imposition at all," he replied, his voice low and husky as he indulged in her touch. "But I have to get up in a few minutes to get ready to head off to work."

"I know."

He felt her push him onto his back before she straddled him and leaned down to kiss him deeply.

"This isn't helping me to get out of bed," Tom said, grinning.

"Who said anything about getting out of bed? You said you had to get up, and I'm helping you with that."

He laughed softly at her. "Nice play on words but," he said as he moved so that she rolled off him. "I am really lucky to have this job and I always have to be on time for it."

Cat nodded, becoming serious. "I know. I promise to be good every morning so you can be at work on time, without any early morning distractions," she said, sitting up and taking off her t-shirt. The mock look of extreme innocence finished off the look she seemed to be trying to achieve.

Tom groaned and forced himself out of bed. "Have I told you how crazy you make me?" he asked, looking at her, topless and looking extremely glorious first thing in the morning. He leaned over and kissed her lips before kissing one nipple and then the other. "Hmm. That image is going to stay with me all day now."

He walked out, definitely needing to get into the shower.

~ ~ ~

Once at work, the day progressed as normal. It was almost possible to forget home as the day got busy and they had times where the customer lines were long. When it was quiet, he asked Toby if he knew of any lawyers.

"Tom, you have a lawyer who is almost part of your family," he said but saw confusion on Tom's face. "Tessa! She is in the legal field. She usually comes in around three today so you might see her. Ask her to help you. I'm sure she will, gladly."

Later in the day, as expected, Tom saw Tessa walk in. As she did, for the first time Tom noticed the small baby bump beginning to show. He was going to be an uncle. That was pretty exciting really. His cousin Daniel had told him that there were Santinis scattered all around Australia but generally, his immediate family was small. He only knew his own family at home plus a few cousins in neighboring areas. The rest he'd never met. It would be nice to see another generation beginning.

"Hello, Tom. How are you going?" Tessa asked in her usual chirpy manner.

"Actually, I was wondering if I could discuss a private matter with you," he said and immediately her attention was captured. "Not here though. How would you feel about coming to my home after I finish here? Sorry to ask but…"

"No! Tom, don't apologize. I am happy to help you, however I can. And I can certainly come to your home. I haven't been there for a while so it would be nice to say hello to your mother," she said, surprising Tom. "Yes, I have met her, and yes I would like to see her again."

"Okay. Thanks. But now, what would you like right now?"

"Hmm, I think I'm going with your Banana Choc Crunch smoothie today. I'm in the mood for something sweet."

"Coming right up."

~ ~ ~

When Tessa entered the Santini family home that evening she was welcomed by Tom and Graham's mother, Victoria. She was also surprised to see Cat Cullen there.

"I thought you were only passing through town when I saw you in the café," Tessa said, expressing her confusion.

"Yes, it's hard for me to know what I'm doing at the moment," Cat responded and then heard Tom speak up.

"Tessa, Cat needs help and advice. Can you help?"

Cat saw Tessa nod slowly. "What can I help you with?"

"Perhaps you two would like to go upstairs into my room and talk there," Tom offered and both women nodded before leaving the room.

"Now, tell me what is happening, Cat," Tessa encouraged as she sat on the bed in the room.

"My ex-husband - Tony - and I separated over a year ago and I had him served with divorce papers…"

"And he won't sign?"

"That is one aspect of it but if that were all there were, I wouldn't be in the position I'm in. He keeps following me and trying to force me to go back with him. Lately, I've been hiding from him in the house of a friend. Well, I *thought* they were my friend until Tony turned up last night. I think it was my so-called 'friend' who told him I was there. I was scared last night, so I ran down the beach from the house and hid," Cat said, opting to leave Tom out of it for the time being, just in case. "I was invited to stay here so I did, but Tessa, what can I do to stop him from coming after me?"

"Have you filed a restraining order against him?" Tessa asked and saw Cat nod. "Good. First stop is for you to file a report with the police…"

"But he's my husband…"

"It doesn't matter," Tessa replied. "Not these days. Maybe five decades ago there was still freedom for a husband to do whatever he wanted to his wife but not now! If there is a restraining order against him then he has broken it and the police need to know."

"But what does it *do?* It doesn't stop him from coming after me," Cat said, the frustration evident in her voice.

"No, but it does give the police reason to act immediately if you ring them and tell them he is near you," Tessa said. "Are you going back to the house you've been staying at?"

Cat shook her head, fear evident on her face. "I gladly leave my stuff behind rather than risk leading him here, or anywhere else."

"Speaking of which," Tessa said with a slight grin on her face. "How did you go from seeing Tom in the café, to staying in his house? I am sure there is a bit of a story there."

She saw Cat nod and smile. "He has been very kind to me."

Tessa laughed. "I *bet* he has! I saw the way he was looking at you, and you at him." She smirked but Cat could read that it was done in friendliness and not in dislike or disapproval. "I haven't known him long but I do think Tom is a good man. Certainly, I'm quite fond of his brother, in case you haven't noticed," she said, letting her hands move over the slight bump beginning to show over her belly. The two women laughed together before Tessa became serious again. "Now, as for you needing to divorce, since you have been separated for a year you can force the issue. When did you have the restraining order placed on him?"

"Just after I left. About thirteen or fourteen months ago, I suppose," Cat replied.

"Good! That will make it easier. It will act as proof that you shouldn't be forced to stay married to him. Can I ask what he did to facilitate the separation? Was he violent toward you?"

"No, to be honest Tessa, when we were living in the same house together he always smiled and charmed. It was when I found out he'd been cheating on me with other women that I decided to leave him. It's since I left that he seems to have become obsessed with me going back to him. Constantly over the last year he's called, sent texts and emails, and at different times found me and tried to drag me back. I just want it to stop."

Tessa looked thoughtful. "I don't know what Tom has told you about his situation…"

"I know that he was in jail for killing a boy."

"Hmm. It is a horrid situation, that one. But Cat, he can't be involved in this. All it would take is for him to punch your ex or do something stupid like that and he could be sent straight back to prison."

Cat nodded. "I know. That is why I am asking for your help. I don't want him involved in this. I just want my life back, to start over."

Tessa smiled. "Those words I've heard before, from Tom. I can see that the two of you would be good for each other."

"Tessa, I'm sorry I lied to you the other day, in the café," Cat said.

"Think nothing of it. You are trying to escape a man who doesn't want to let you go. If I were in that position I wouldn't be telling the truth of what I was doing either. Your focus needs to be on keeping safe, Cat. And enjoying that man downstairs … if that is what is going on…?" she asked semi-discretely and saw Cat blush and nod.

"I do like him … a lot."

"I get that. I think both Santini brothers have a charm that makes us women want to fall at their feet."

"How did you meet Graham?"

"I was a prosecutor on a case in court and Graham was the defense lawyer. When I walked into court and saw him I just about fell over, he was just so gorgeous. It made my job all that much harder but once I refocused I was able to do it better."

"But how does your work not affect the two of you together, if you are on opposite sides of the law, with you helping put people away and him trying to keep them free?"

Tessa laughed softly. "Fortunately, that case was a one-off. I am not a full-time prosecutor and to be honest, I don't like being in the courtroom. I'd much rather do the behind the scenes legal work. So our jobs haven't overlapped since that one case. *And* I am going to give up work in a few months. I don't want the stress of my job interfering with my trying to be a good mother."

"I am sure you will be a great mother, Tessa," Cat said, feeling a little saddened that she had missed the mark with Tony and the happy ever after she had thought she'd get with him was never going to happen. In that, she had been fooled. Silently she was glad no children had been born. It would have made her current circumstance that much harder to bear if they were also having to run from him.

"Thank you. Now, so, tonight, stay here if you can. Are Tom and his mother happy for you to stay here? Because I have a spare room at my place…"

"Oh, no, I think Tom was sincere when he said I could stay here."

"Alright. Tomorrow morning I will go talk to the local police and make it known to them that you have a restraining order and your ex is following you. Do you happen to have the restraining order with you?"

Cat shook her head, regretful at not making sure she had it on her at all times.

"That's okay. They will be able to give me a copy of it anyway, and I'll get a verified copy for you to have. What about a photo of him?"

"Um, I did have some in my phone but I think I deleted them," Cat said, taking her phone out of her pocket and scrolling through the photo album. "No, wait, I still have this one."

Tessa saw the phone held up and looked at the man, trying to memorize his face. "Can you text it to me? I'll show it to the police so they can have it on record."

"Do you really think any of this will make a difference, Tessa? I don't understand why he keeps coming after me. If he was happy with me, he wouldn't have cheated. I know that. Why can't he see that?"

"I don't know but I'll do what I can to help you. For now, though, keep a low profile. I can pick things up for you if you want. I work right in the centre of town so nothing is too far to go for."

"Thank you. Tom offered that as well."

Tessa looked at her and smiled. "I'm thinking you might have a soft spot for Tom. Am I right in that assumption?"

She saw Cat blush slightly before nodding.

"I feel like I've met someone I'm in tune with. I didn't feel like that even with Tony. But this thing with Tom is new, too. Things are always shiny when they're new, right? Over time they always start to lose their shine until they become dull."

"He isn't going to become dull. Trust me as another woman involved with a Santini boy!"

Tessa said, grinning. "Now, I must get going but I will find a way to contact you when I have some useful news. I think you should get rid of that phone though, Cat, and the SIM card. Do you want me to pick up a new one for you tomorrow?"

Cat instantly turned her phone off, not having thought about it previously.

"If that's possible, that would be great. I have some cash here that should get the cheapest one anyway. That's all I need, Tessa. No bells and whistles. Just a phone I can use as a phone."

"No problem. I might pop back in tomorrow night. I'll see how I go for time."

Cat walked downstairs with her and the two women entered the living room where Tom sat with his mother.

"Is everything alright?" he asked and saw both nod.

"Yes, but I have to go. It was nice seeing you again Tom. And you, Mrs Santini."

"Victoria! I keep telling you, Tessa. Call me Victoria!"

Tessa smiled and nodded. "Alright, Victoria. Goodnight."

~ ~ ~

Later that night as Tom held her in his arms, Cat found herself believing in a happier ever after than what she had believed possible only days earlier. Who knew where things with Tom would go. Perhaps nowhere. For the present moment, however, he was right there, holding her and helping her feel secure. Lying next to him, she was aware of the feelings awake inside of her due to him being so close. She wanted him so much but wouldn't push him. Her body was trying to win out over respect. In that regard, her head was stronger. She would only be respectful to the woman who was letting her stay in her home, in her son's bed. It wasn't easy lying so close to him and not touching him but restraint was doable. They could have their intimate times once it was all finished with and she was finally free.

As her mind churned over, full of those thoughts, Tom's was focused on the smell of her and the sound of her light breath. He was trying not to think about her soft breasts that were pressing against his chest. He also wasn't trying to think about her mouth, or her hands, or her thighs, or her … any other part of her body. The more he tried to not think about those things, the more he did. He quietly wondered how couples slept next to each other night after night for the rest of their lives. He felt like he was *bursting* to touch her.

"Is your mind too active to sleep?" Cat asked him as she sensed tenseness in his body.

"I'm trying to control my arousal … again," he said and heard her laugh quietly. "I never thought I could be like this around anyone, Cat. It actually feels like my body needs yours. Almost like it's pining for it, in its absence."

"It's right here, you know," Cat teased. "With me."

Tom chuckled softly. "I know, but as difficult as it is, I would rather wait than…"

She put her hand on his chest and kissed his lips softly. "I agree."

He pulled her close and eventually, after much not thinking about her beautiful lips, hands and body, he finally found peace as he slipped into a deep slumber.

CHAPTER 7

Tessa, in a quiet moment of the following day, visited the police to talk to them about Cat's situation and obtain a copy of the restraining order. She then went to purchase a new mobile phone for Cat. In her office, she poured through her legal documentation to determine the legalities of Cat being able to divorce from a man who seemed set on not letting that happen.

After work, she cautiously drove to Tom's home. She had considered dropping the items off to him at the café but felt good about going to see Cat in person instead. She could probably use all the friends she had, given that at least one of her friends had proven to be anything but when she'd told Tony where Cat was staying.

The phone was dropped off and Tessa joined them for dinner. Finally, the conversation moved from serious to light-hearted. For hours, Tom, Cat, Tessa and Victoria swapped stories from childhood through to the present day, making them all laugh and for the moment forget their worries.

It was after 11pm when Tessa finally left so that the household could get to bed. When she was in

114

her car home, her mobile rang. It was the Chief of Police, who she had visited that morning. Seeing his name on her phone screen, she pulled her car over and answered.

"Tessa, that guy you were doing research on today..."

"Tony O'Malley?"

"Yes. I just wanted you to know that he's been in an accident. He didn't make it."

Tessa sat quiet, in shock. "Tony O'Malley is dead?"

"Yes."

"You're sure?"

"No doubt about it. And now I'm thinking, with your questions this morning, that perhaps the wife..."

"I've been with her all evening, Chief."

"You have?"

"Yes, I went to the house where she is staying, early, about five o'clock, and I am literally on my way home now. I left there only five or ten minutes ago. I am telling you, she was there the whole evening."

"Alright, well if you say you were with her, I might need to talk to you again."

"If you are asking questions like that, his death must be suspicious..."

"I'll talk to you when I have more information. But Tessa..."

"Yes?"

"Tell your friend not to leave town. I will definitely be talking to her."

Tessa heard the phone call end and sat still in her car, not moving, for a long while. The man she had been eager to help fight was dead. He was no longer a threat to anyone. It was an easy way out for Cat. Was it *too* easy a way out for her though? Sure, she had been there in the house tonight, but *could* she have had anything to do with his death? And if so, was Tom about to be dragged through the police system again?

She started her car. After briefly considering driving back to the house and informing everyone there that he was dead, she decided against it. Tomorrow things might get crazy for Cat and Tom. Tonight they should have peace and the comfort of each other, without anything more to worry about.

~ ~ ~

The next morning Tessa went to the station and spoke to the Chief of Police again.

"We need to talk to the wife, but we don't know where she is. Do you?" he asked her and she nodded. "She needs to come in to see us."

"How did he die?"

"Tessa, you know I can't share that with you. Not until our investigation is complete."

She nodded to acknowledge she did understand.

"I know. It was worth a try though."

He smiled at her. "I like you, Tessa. You *are* one for trying. Now go and tell her to come and see us, before we have to go and drag her here."

"I'm on it."

Tessa got in her car and immediately drove to Tom's parents' house. She referred to it as that but in all honesty, she had never even seen Mr Santini Senior. Graham refused to talk about him, and Tom and Victoria simply never mentioned him. It was as if he didn't even exist. She wondered if he even had any idea what amazing men his sons were, or if knew he was going to become a grandfather in the coming months. Thinking about that, she placed a protective hand on her belly. The bump wasn't large yet. It was at the stage where it was visible in some clothing but not in others. As she thought about her baby slowly growing inside of her, she thought about the little one's father.

She missed Graham. She wanted to talk to him, to hear his voice. She wanted to see his handsome face and feel his arms around her. She wished he hadn't gone away. She wanted him home.

For now, she had news to deliver. After knocking on the door to Tom's family home, she was let in by Victoria, who told her Cat was sitting in the back yard, enjoying some sunshine.

Making her way out to the back garden area,

Tessa considered the ways she could break the news. Assuming Cat didn't already know, of course. Perhaps she should find that out first.

"Good morning," she called out and immediately saw Cat smile and stand.

"What are you doing here?" Cat asked. "You have already done so much for me, Tessa!"

"I wanted to see how you are feeling, first of all. Are you alright?"

"Yes, I'm fine. I know I might have to leave again, to find somewhere new to hide, so I'm just trying to enjoy this while I can. It's so nice and peaceful here."

"Cat, there *is* another reason I've come this morning. The police want to talk to you, and I said I'd give you a ride to the station. Could you come now?"

"Of … of course. Is everything alright? Is it something to do with the restraining order?"

"I think it best that they talk to you, rather than me," Tessa replied. "But it *is* advisable that you go."

"Alright. I'll just freshen up and then we'll go."

Cat was nervous and apprehensive but smiled and went to wash her hands. Nothing more was said as Tessa drove them to the police station.

"I can't come in with you, but I'll be waiting for you to call me if you want to when you come out. My number is in your phone," Tessa said.

Cat nodded, experiencing a feeling of dread roll over her. She made her way into the station, gave her name and was soon in a small room with one table and three chairs. One on her side of the table. Two on the other. Facing her was the police chief and another officer.

"Where were you last night between seven and nine, Mrs O'Malley?"

"Oh, I was at a friend's house. Why? What is this about?"

"And this friend could verify that you were there?"

"Yes," Cat replied, nodding. "There were four of us there till close to midnight, and then one left. I stayed there all night until this morning when I've come here."

Cat watched the faces of the men before her. She was becoming morc and more nervous by the second.

"What was your relationship with your husband like?"

"What? Oh, we were separated. We split up over a year ago," Cat said. "Since then I've been moving around, trying to start over."

"And?"

"And he's been following me ever since I left. I took out a restraining order but I don't think it means anything to him."

She saw the senior officer nod before the

questions continued.

"When did you last see or hear from your husband, Mrs O'Malley?"

"Two nights ago. He turned up at the house I was staying in, and tried to get me to leave with him."

"What happened?"

"When he reached a certain point of anger and I saw a chance to, I ran. I ran out the back door and along the beach, and hid behind a large rock until I thought he had gone. That was the last time I saw him." She waited as both officers took notes. "Please, what is this about? Is it about the restraining order? Can you do anything to stop him from following me?"

"Mrs O'Malley, your husband won't be following you anymore. Do you know why?"

She heard the question and was alarmed. Partly by the news and more so by the way the officers were looking at her. It suddenly felt as if the next words that came out of her mouth could potentially be the most important words she ever spoke in her life.

"No. Has he done something? Is he locked up? What is going *on?*"

"Your husband is dead, Mrs O'Malley. He was found deceased last night."

Cat heard the words but it took a moment for her to process them. "What? But … how?

Where?"

"We can't share that information with you right now."

Still the lengthy stares continued like they were inspecting her as if she were an alien being they had never seen. She was aware of them watching for every action and every reaction.

"Did you want your husband killed?"

"No!" Cat exclaimed, horrified. "I wanted him to just leave me alone! No, of *course* I didn't want him dead. He treated me badly and I wanted to be away from him but I don't think he deserved to *die!*"

"Who do you think would have wanted to kill him?"

"I don't know. I don't know what his life was like for the past year, except for the times where he was messaging and following me. I wouldn't know what else he did," Cat replied as she felt weariness flow over her. "He made sure that all of our mutual friends stayed on his side when I left. Everyone had to be *his* friend. I walked away with only one who I trusted, and she betrayed me by telling him where I was. So, no, I can't help you with that. He did have lovers, though, and I know at least some of them were ongoing. You could try asking them. They might have had a better idea about what he was doing."

"I'll need names," the chief said, pushing a pen

and paper toward her.

"Names? Of my husband's lovers? Are you *serious?* How could I know the names of all the women my ex slept with?!"

"You know that he was with women. Just write down any details you can remember. First names, where they might have lived, where you think they met up for their encounters."

The word hung in the air. 'Encounters.' Was that what it was called when someone's husband ran into the arms of another woman? An encounter?

Cat took her time to think. She could remember the face of one she'd seen, and she could remember the motel she'd seen him walking out of with a different woman on his arm. That was it. Shortly after she'd seen that, she'd left, hoping to never see his face again. Regardless, she wrote down what she could remember, even with it being vague.

"Thank you," the officer said as Cat pushed the paper back to him. "Are you his next of kin?"

She was alarmed at the question and startled at not knowing the answer. "I don't know. Am I? I doubt it. Why would I be, if we were separated and heading for divorce? His parents are still alive and should be contacted. I can't say what importance he placed on the women."

The officer nodded. "We will contact Mr and Mrs O'Malley shortly and we will check out these details you have given us. We need you to stay in town for now, Mrs O'Malley."

"Yes, of course. I had no set plans to leave, but please don't call me by my married name. I prefer to use my maiden name, Cat Cullen."

The officers nodded and stood, ending the interrogation before escorting her out to the front of the station.

"We'll be in touch."

That was that. Cat had just learned that her ex was dead. He would no longer be sending her messages. He would no longer be calling her. He would no longer be turning up wherever she was, demanding that she go home with him - wherever it was that he meant by 'home'. It was over. She should breathe a sigh of relief but she had spent time with him earlier on that had been good. The news that his life had ended didn't bring her joy at all.

Feeling alone and tears coming on she looked around, spotted a children's playground and walked over to it to sit on a swing. There, she didn't hold back. Tony was dead. He'd been an asshole, but she never wanted that for him. He'd been healthy, as far as she knew, so that, combined with the questions the police had asked, made her think that his death must be suspicious. What had he done that could have driven someone to do that to him?

~ ~ ~

Tessa walked into the café just before lunchtime. She was glad to see it empty in the pre-lunch build up. As soon as she entered she saw Tom's eyes change, as if he were expecting bad news.

"What is it? Has something happened to Cat?" he asked.

"No, but…"

"But what?"

"Tom, I took her to the police station," Tessa said. "Her husband was found dead last night."

Tom heard the words and was stunned into silence. He'd only seen Tony two nights earlier. How could the guy be dead?

"I … I don't understand," he said.

"The police are talking to Cat right now. They know she was with me last night so there shouldn't be any problem, I don't think…"

"I have to go," he started to say, looking as if he were beginning to panic.

Tessa held out her hands as an attempt to stop him.

"No, wait! Tom, you can't barge in there. Please let me advise you on this as a lawyer and as a friend. You need to stay where you are and not do *anything*. They will come and talk to you, too, I have no doubt. Don't make things worse by reacting and doing something that will make you the highlight of their focus."

Tom stood still and absorbed what she was saying. He knew she was right. He couldn't risk putting himself in the spotlight in front of the police. Even with the circumstances of how he'd come to be in prison, he was still a man who had been convicted of manslaughter. He could still be an obvious choice of suspect if Tony really were dead.

He felt anger flow through his body. If he were a violent man, he would have right then punched a hole in the wall. Instead, he calmed himself and nodded.

"I know you're right. I won't do anything."

She looked closely at him and believed his words to be true. He and Graham were so different as brothers, and yet in some ways so similar. She missed Graham. She missed him deeply and hoped he would come home soon.

"I have to go back to work," she said. "If the police come to talk to you, keep calm! They will only be asking routine questions."

Tom nodded again. "I'll be fine. Thank you."

He watched as she walked out of the café, wondering how his brother could have left town and left her. What was he doing in Brisbane, to take him away from the woman he loved, who was having his baby?

As customers filed in, the thought was

forgotten.

~ ~ ~

Cat made her way back to the beach and walked along the length of it before she found a spot in the sunshine. There she sat down on the sand and looked out over the ocean. Her emotions were tugging at her, pulling her in conflicting directions. She was free from him finally, but he was dead. Was that a fair trade-off? Really? His life was over. No matter what he'd put her through and how much hurt she'd felt from his actions, she cried for him. They had shared some good times - *many* good times at the very start. Those memories had been overshadowed in recent times by his persistence in pursuing her. But the memories were still there and now that he was gone, wasn't it better to focus on the good times, rather than the bad?

She wept for a long time. Whether all due to sadness or partially due to relief as stress finally released from her body, she did not know. All that she could focus on at that moment was the fact that it felt good to cry. Anything could happen in the coming days and weeks. Would she have to identify his body? Would she have to handle any affairs of his finances or home? She had been removed from his life for so long that she didn't know anything about any of that anymore. She found herself hoping that he had left a will that left all decisions and assets to someone else. She didn't want to deal with any of it. She just wanted to start a new life.

Late in the afternoon, as the sun was beginning to fade, she felt the presence of someone sit down beside her. Turning, she saw Tom.

"Shouldn't you be at work?" she asked.

Tom laughed softly at her while taking her hand in his. "I was. I've been there all day. It's getting late. How long have you been sitting here?"

"I'm not sure. Probably hours I suppose."

He lifted her hand and kissed it. "How are you feeling about what's happened?"

"Mixed, really. I wanted to be away from him forever, but I do feel sad, Tom. He wasn't a good husband, but he *was* my husband. I married him because I loved him and I truly believed that he and I had a future together. It is hard to believe that he's gone."

"Did the police say anything about what happened?" he asked and saw her shake her head slowly.

"No, they said they can't disclose that. I suppose it doesn't matter. The result is still the same, isn't it."

Tom put his arm around her shoulder and pulled her close. There they sat, looking out over the ocean, as the sun slowly but finally made its way down and below the horizon.

"It's getting cold," Tom said. "Do you want to come home with me?"

Cat looked at him in surprise. It hadn't occurred to her to go anywhere else.

"Of course. If I'm still welcome. If not…"

He kissed her, deeply and passionately, cutting off the sentence that almost left her lips. Her very, very kissable lips.

"Or perhaps…" she started to say in a low whisper, her mind getting fuzzy from his kisses.

"Or perhaps what?"

"How would you feel about us checking into a motel for the night? I know your mother is at home alone so I understand if it isn't a good idea…"

Once more his lips crushed down onto hers as she was mid-sentence. The kissing grew and matured as his tongue pushed into her mouth and started its dance with her tongue. Her body pressed hard against his and he wrapped his arms around her as tightly as he could. When he heard her groan in happiness and arousal he pulled away abruptly, feeling like he was at breaking point.

"Wait," Tom said. "I'll call Toby and see if I can have tomorrow morning off work first."

Cat waited patiently as she heard him make the call and then end it with a large smile on his face. "No work tomorrow at all. Come on," he said and immediately held out his hand to invite her to take it in her own. "I'll stop in at home to tell Mom what I'm doing, just to make sure she doesn't worry, and then we'll go."

Cat laughed at him although he could still hear sadness in her tone.

"But where will we go, Tom?"

"Anywhere that has a room spare, if you agree. I don't care about luxury or a view or anything else like that right now. I just want to be alone with you - just the two of us - just for a while."

He saw her nod and smile in agreement.

~ ~ ~

After grabbing what he needed and telling his mother of their plans, they found their way to a motel on the outskirts of the city. It wasn't the most beautiful place but the room was warm and dry and the bed was big. It wouldn't have mattered what it looked like. The moment the door was closed, Cat moved to him and embraced him, inviting him to put his arms around her in return.

"Do you still want to take things slow?" she asked him, breathless, between kisses.

"Hell, no!" he replied, making her laugh. There was a part of her that wouldn't be completely happy tonight. She pushed that down for the moment and focused on the part of her that still could be.

Cat encouraged him to undress her and he did so with care and adoration in his eyes. As soon as he had removed her last piece of clothing, she lay back on the bed and watched as he peeled his own layers off, revealing the body she had been dreaming of over the previous two nights. He was so beautifully proportioned and toned. The combination of that with his day-old stubble covering his jaw made him downright irresistible.

Tom climbed onto the bed and lay on top of her to kiss her, fighting to not rush. Even though he'd been shy and had needed her to lead the way the previous time they had been together, something seemed to have changed in him. He confidently took the lead and made her body shiver in delightful waves of climax through his efforts before he plunged deep into her. The volume and tone of her moans pushed him on and he was soon thrusting hard into her before that place was reached - that wonderful, all-consuming place of passion that was like no other.

"Not the shy boy now, I see," Cat said, teasing him as they lay in each other's arms afterward.

Tom smiled at her and kissed her softly. "Well, I still have a lot of practice to do to perfect anything."

She laughed out loud at him and he shivered at the sound. There was so much potential for her to be happy, but he knew she must be full of stress. Having an ex follow and pursue her was one thing. Knowing he'd been killed was another.

Tom pulled her into his arms and they lay together, silent, for a long while.

"I know it's not a permanent solution to anything, but it feels good to be here with you. Thank you," she said and immediately felt his lips touch her forehead.

"It was a good idea," Tom replied. "It's nice sleeping next to you night after night but seeing you like this, lying gloriously naked on top of this bed, is something I'm definitely not against experiencing more often." He pulled away far enough so that he could look at her. "You affect me so much, Cat." He paused for a long while before he found the courage to speak again. "Will you stay in town now?"

She smiled at him sadly. Plans - that was what he was asking about, but what could she tell him?

"I don't know what will happen now, Tom. I have to be here while the police do whatever it is that they're doing, I suppose. There isn't any way for me to make plans until this is all over. I'm not even sure if I'm Tony's next of kin. I assume not but I don't *know*. I might have to arrange his funeral, or I might not." She looked deeply into his eyes and ran her fingers through his hair. "We can't make definite plans, but I do know that if I can work things so that I can stay in town, and still be with you, that *is* what I'll do. I just don't want to make you any promises when I don't even know…"

He leaned in and kissed her. "I understand. No promises."

Cat pushed him onto his back and positioned herself over him, loving the way his hands naturally moved to her hips and over her back as they kissed. Lying like that, straddling him, feeling his hands on her and enjoying the entwinement of their lips and tongues together, she wondered how she could ever think of leaving. He was a beautiful man and whenever she was with him she felt fire in the veins throughout her entire body. But even more than that, she knew he was a good man who would never cause anyone any harm if he could help it. His soul was kind.

Tom watched her move on him. She was in the zone - the one where he could sense her heading toward orgasm. Her face said so much to him when she was like that and her beauty was breathtaking. Not just her face, but her body. As it moved, his eyes roamed up and down the length of her torso. Her breasts were beautiful - not too large but definitely a perfect shape to fit his hand. Her belly had just a slight curve to it - blissfully not tabletop flat but far more human and relaxed than that. And down, to the natural hair that she didn't seem to have ever shaved to be rid of. All of her as a package was beautiful, physically. But it was the combination of what she looked like and her personality that tipped him over the edge in wanting to keep knowing her if it were going to be possible. She was intriguing. He hoped their journey had only just begun.

When he heard, felt and saw her body clench in climax, he let himself go and Cat felt it through her own shimmers of delight. She let her body slump down on him and had no desire to move.

After a long while, they readied for sleep and Tom happily wrapped himself around her and held her close. As he heard her breathing change, indicating to him she'd fallen into slumber, he lay awake and thought about the circumstances they were in. He didn't want to think about it but he knew he was in a dangerous place. For him not to be considered a suspect would have to be some kind of miracle, and he had fear inside of him. He didn't want to go back to jail … never at all, under any circumstances, but especially for something he didn't do.

~ ~ ~

"Good morning," he heard her soft voice say as he turned over in the haziness of waking.

Upon opening his eyes, he saw her lying on her side, facing him and smiling. He smiled back and let his eyes wander over her. She was under the covers - *most* of her was under the covers. He couldn't have avoided noticing her breasts were uncovered, even if he had wanted to pretend so. She was quite a vision.

"I think I've woken in heaven," he said and saw her chuckle before she moved closer to him so that he could put his arm around her. "Good morning to you too, Foxy Cat."

Hearing him greet her in such a way, particularly first thing in the morning, produced a feeling of security in Cat. She'd known him for so little time and yet lying beside him, sleeping beside him … making love with him … all felt so natural. So right.

Tom heard her tummy growl and teased her. "Hungry?"

"Yes! I must have burned off some calories last night. Aren't you hungry?" she asked before Tom flipped her onto her back and began moving on top of her.

"I am absolutely starving," he replied before responding to her arms coming around his neck and pulling him to her. There was no mistaking the deep huskiness of his voice or his level of hardness as he pressed between her thighs.

"Should we order some breakfast then?" she teased him between the kisses that were growing in intensity. "I mean, if you're starving…"

She said no more as he kissed her and then moved down her body, tasting all that he wanted to in that particular moment.

~ ~ ~

"We have to check out shortly," Cat said as they lay back on the bed a long time later. They had made love, eaten room service breakfast, showered together, and then made each other smile one more time.

"We do," Tom replied, for the moment enjoying just lying still and not doing anything. He was sated after an amazing night and a grand morning of desire and pleasure. Soon they would have to return to reality. When they stepped outside the hotel door, anything could happen. For all he knew, the police could be eagerly waiting to see him. Waiting to question him. Waiting to move him into the main role of the prime suspect on a centre stage.

"Come on then, Lovely Tom," Cat said, giggling as she tried to think of an equal name to his name for her. "Or Large Tom? Long Tom? Lusty Tom?"

He watched her giggle and couldn't help but smile and then laugh at her. For the moment, his worries were forgotten.

~ ~ ~

On the journey back to Tom's family home, Cat's phone rang and she eagerly answered it.

"Tessa. What's happened?" she asked, her voice revealing her degree of concern about everything going on. "What? I don't understand. Are you sure? That can't be … yes, alright. I'll tell him. Thank you for calling. Bye."

After she hung up, Tom eagerly waited for some news to come. When none came, he prompted her. "What did Tessa say?"

Cat turned to face him, feeling heavily in shock. "I do have news but I'll hold onto it until you've stopped driving."

Tom heard the words and immediately assessed where he could pull over safely. Once the car had stopped, he removed his seatbelt and turned his body fully to face her front on. His heart was racing in fear of what was coming.

"Tessa said that … the police have stopped investigating," she said and then paused before continuing. "They … they've made a public announcement that they have indisputable evidence about who killed Tony. They have her in custody."

"Her?"

Tom saw Cat nod, the surprise or shock evident on her face. "Tracy. The friend of mine who let me stay in her house on the beach. They've arrested her for his murder."

The news forcefully rushed around inside of Tom's head. He'd been so focused on hearing that he had to go in to be questioned that he now found it difficult to refocus on what the truth was.

"Wait. Your friend invited you to stay in her

house to get away from Tony? And then she told Tony where you were? And then she ... killed him?"

To each of his questions, Cat had nodded.

"But why?" Tom asked. The information made no sense.

"I ... I don't know," Cat replied. "I suppose the police will talk to me and tell me? Will they? I don't even know ... oh, it's so frustrating not knowing where I actually stand in this whole mess!"

"Well, what else did Tessa say? Did the police tell her that they would need to talk to you again?"

"She didn't say," Cat replied, shaking her head. "But she did say that the police are releasing the body - *Tony* - to his parents. I assume they will take care of his funeral."

The two of them sat in silence, processing the information. Inside of Tom's head rested relief for himself, but frustration for Cat. Inside of Cat's head was confusion. Was she a widow or an ex-wife? Was she both? With Tony having died, where did she stand as having been his wife, and still being his wife on paper, but having been separated from him for more than a year?

"Do you want to go to the police station?" Tom asked her after a long period of silence.

"No. His parents need to handle everything and I don't want to interrupt their process of doing that. If the police need to talk to me, they will come and find me."

Tom waited to see if she would say anything more. While he sat there, he looked at her closely. Her confusion was great. That was completely obvious on her face. She was also incredibly beautiful. That thought he tried to push down and not be at the forefront of his mind. Now was not the right time to be thinking about their time together the night before or that morning.

"We can go, Tom. I don't have anything more to report about what Tessa said."

                    CHAPTER 8

Over the following days, Tom returned to work as
normal and Cat remained in the Santini family
home. The police had called her into the station
and informed her of their arrest, although they
wouldn't give her any explanation or reason for
the murder. Tony's parents had identified their
son's body and insisted he go with them to be
buried in their family plot. They had requested
that Cat not be told about the funeral because they
did not want her there. When Cat heard that news
she was sad but understood. No matter how she
was in their marriage, she was sure Tony would
have twisted everything around so that all that
was bad appeared to be her fault. She could not
imagine his parents knew about the women he'd
had on the side of their marriage, and she
certainly had no intention of telling them. Let
them continue to regard their son as an angel, and
her as the one who ruined his marriage. Knowing
that it wasn't the truth was good enough for Cat.
Now she had to start thinking just about herself.
Tony's death wasn't the circumstance that she
would have liked to have become so but finally,
she was safe. She could step out into the sunshine

once more and do whatever she wanted, without fear he would come after her. But she had been hiding behind that excuse for not living, for so long, that she could hardly think about what she wanted to do that day, let alone the rest of her life.

During the days when Tom worked, Cat helped his mother with things around the home and spent time with Tessa. Each afternoon, after he'd finished work, Tom would find her sitting on the sand at the beach, looking out toward the horizon. He knew she was now relieved and stress-free, but he also saw in her a deep level of sadness. That part of her he wouldn't try to reach. It was sacred and only she could change it herself, within her. He'd had times like that when he'd first been released from prison but he'd slowly come right and then he'd met her. Since that moment, seeing her come into the café with her dress soaked through from the rain, his feelings had grown intensely. Yes, she enflamed his desire, but there was so much more to her than that. She was kind and giving, and right from when he'd revealed his past to her, she had been able to look beyond that and focus solely on who he was as a man in the present.

Each afternoon when he saw her on the beach after he finished work, he thought that she seemed a little more animated than she had the day before. She had things on her mind that she needed to work through, but slowly she did seem to be confronting them and working through them.

"How is my Foxy Cat today?" he asked her one day as he sat beside her on the warmed sand.

When Cat turned to him he saw yet another level of regained life. "I got a job today."

He looked at her, surprised. "You did? Well, that's great. What is it?"

Suddenly her eyes took on a new level of life again and her face became more than animated. It was easy for Tom to see she was really excited.

"Receptionist at the hospital. It's similar to the job I had before I got married," she said, full of life. "I worked in a job like that for five years and I loved it so much. Getting to talk to patients and their loved ones always felt like I could make a little difference by helping them in whatever way I could. I need that now. I've been so caught up in hiding from Tony that I've built myself into some weird cocoon, but I want to help other people and this is a start."

Her words made Tom think back to when he'd gotten the café job with Toby. To so many people it would be an insignificant job but to him it was important. He wanted to work hard and slowly he was getting to know people. He knew the power of just smiling at someone, greeting them and not only asking them how their day was going, but truly listening to their answer. People sometimes needed that. They needed just one person to really show an interest.

Cat looked intently at Tom and saw him smile broadly at her.

"I am really happy for you and I can see how happy you are about it."

"It's time for me to start living a normal life again," she said quietly and turned her gaze out to the water for a long while before she turned her attention back to him. "How was your day in the café?"

"Good. Busy," Tom replied. "My brother, Graham, came in to let me know he's back in town. It was good to see and talk to him for a while."

"Oh, that's good. I know Tessa has been missing him. Will I get to meet him?"

Tom smiled at her, loving the sense of easiness suddenly flowing from her. "Of course you will. The two lovebirds might need some time together first but I'm sure when they're ready to emerge from their little bubble, we'll see them."

He watched her face and enjoyed having her move closer to him to press her lips against his. It was probably meant to be a light passing-by kiss but it deepened and Tom soon found himself wrapped up in her … and around her … as they lay on the beach.

"You know this is a family-friendly spot,

right?" he teased her and she smiled at him.

"I know. But no-one's around right now…"

He laughed and gently nudged her off him. "Stop that thinking, Foxy Cat! It's hard enough to control myself around you as it is." She watched as he stood up fully and leaned down with his hand outstretched. "Come on. Let's walk along the beach for a while."

As she stood up, she held his hand to stop him from moving away and pulled so that both of them came together, chest to chest. She wrapped her arms around him, loving the feeling of security that always came from being in his arms. Tom wrapped his arms around her in return, happy to be able to hold her and comfort her.

"Do you have the next two days off?" she asked and saw him nod.

"I do. When do you start your job?"

"Day after tomorrow."

"So we are both free all day tomorrow?" he asked and she smiled and nodded at him. "You look like you might have something on your mind. Something you would like us to do tomorrow," he teased her. "Come on. Out with it."

Cat pulled away from him and looked at him closely as she put to him the suggestion that had been on her mind since learning that she was soon to work and earn.

"Tom, what do you think about the idea of you

and me getting our own place? Please don't be offended by my suggestion. I am thankful for having been able to stay at your parents' home but…"

He kissed her deeply. "The idea has crossed my mind too, but there is one huge problem with that though."

Cat sighed deeply, ready for disappointment. Of course he wouldn't want to live with her. Now he was going to let her down softly by making some excuse. Oh well, may as well get it over with and hear what he was going to tell her. She'd survived a horrid marriage and a stalker ex. Really, she could survive anything if she had to.

She looked at him and finally prompted him to move forward with saying whatever was going to rip her heart out. "What would that be?"

"If we are alone in a home together, there is a very good chance that you will never get anything done, since I will always want to have my lips and hands on you."

Cat heard the words and had to let them process in her mind for a while before she fully understood that she wasn't being rejected at all. Throughout her thought process, Tom watched her. He could almost see her different stages of thinking, by the subtle changes in her facial expression. When she finally realized that he was teasing her and he most definitely wasn't rejecting her, he saw her smile at last.

"You aren't saying no?"

"What? Why would I say no? Are you *kidding me?* Cat, you are amazing and you inspire me in ways you don't even seem aware of. I want to be able to spend time with you alone in our own place. The thought of doing things together - cooking, cleaning, dancing ... whatever - is amazing to me."

"Dancing? Cleaning?" she asked, laughing as she felt tears in her eyes. "Seriously? We're going to clean together? And you want to dance?"

He laughed out loud at her, loving the expressiveness of the tear on her cheek.

"Whatever you want, I'm in," he said, grinning.

She reached up and guided his head down to kiss her.

"Do you want to go look at places tomorrow then?"

He nodded and smiled. "Definitely."

CHAPTER 9

The hunt was on. Between them, they had secured five places to look at- two apartments and three standalone cottages.

As they were shown into the first apartment by the agent, Cat gasped. The space before her was large, modern and very shiny. Everywhere she looked there was some kind of gloss - waxed wooden floors, pristine kitchen benchtop and large spotless glass windows.

"Holy….!" Tom exclaimed when they entered. He'd only ever lived in his parents' home, which was cozy and homely. This was at the very far end of the spectrum of homeliness but it was beautiful all the same.

Cat walked around and chatted to the agent. For a moment Tom thought it had caught Cat's attention and this might be the kind of place he might live in with her. Then he heard her speak softly to him.

"I like this, but it isn't really me. What do you think of it?"

He nodded in relief. It was beautiful … for someone else. "I think we should move on to prospect number two."

They thanked the agent and began their journey to the next appointment. The second agent was showing them around a tiny cottage. From the street, it looked very small, especially compared to other larger houses around it. They entered through a wooden gate that seemed to stand direct centre of a long white picket fence. As they walked up the path, on either side of them were flowers. Lots and *lots* of flowers. The smell emanating from them was amazing, making Cat take a deep breath to appreciate it.

Walking forward, they walked up steps to the front door. The wooden veranda that extended along the front of the house had a curved roof overhanging it. Already Tom found the property much more like a home than the apartment they'd just seen.

As they entered the front door, the first things Cat saw were the small home's ornate ceilings and solid timber doorways and architraves.

"Oh!" Tom heard her exclaim and the sound made him smile.

They took their time walking through. It was as tiny inside as it had looked from the outside. When they stepped out the back door, they were overwhelmed by the rear yard.

"There is no way we could afford this, Cat," Tom said, not wanting to break her heart. Even though the home was small, it didn't seem possible that the rent could be cheap. "I don't earn much at the café."

"Actually, the owner has asked for it to be let at a reduced price for the right tenants who will love it and care for it," the agent spoke up. When she told them the price of rent, Cat almost shrieked, making Tom laugh. Now the cost seemed over the top in a reverse way. How could the owners rent it out for so little? "Part of your responsibility for paying only this much will be maintaining the front and back yards. As I am sure you can tell, the owners have put much time and love into their gardens. They do expect whoever rents this place, to continue to keep it looking immaculate and healthy. Oh, and *alive*," she said, with a slight smile at her last comment. "I'll give you guys a few minutes alone to have a chat."

She walked away, leaving Cat and Tom alone. They moved forward to a swing seat and sat down together.

"Is this really something you want, Tom? To live together? Because I can probably rent this place alone…"

He pulled her to him and kissed her. "I'd like to. But let's step away from the romance for a minute and talk practicalities."

She smiled at him but nodded. "Alright. Well, I know I am going to be earning enough to cover the rent myself if I have to."

"If we get this place together, we can split the rent 50/50?" he asked, forcing himself to be realistic and practical for just a few minutes. She nodded.

"Yep, and then we can just split the bills - power, food, whatever. That works for me," she said, excited at the prospect since in her marriage Tony had always insisted he handle everything. Even in the present time, she had no idea what their financial situation had ever been. They had both earned money and he had paid bills. He had controlled everything and she had never questioned that. The idea of having everything equal was a thrilling one to her.

Tom considered the idea. Even though he was 28 years old, he'd only lived in two places - his parents' home and prison. While his family home was certainly much more enjoyable to be in than jail, neither place had been a place of love. That was something he was yet to experience.

He looked at Cat closely. He was in awe of her and he loved being with her but he forced himself to take a moment to consider the two of them living together. There would be good things of course. The only thing that made him question the ease with which he could say yes and actually move in with her, was the limited time they had known each other. It seemed like they had been together for much longer. In reality, it was only a short time and things didn't always go right in his life. He also hated the thought of her being left with an entire house and rent if something went wrong in his life again. But she had just said she could cover the rent herself, hadn't she? Surely that was a sign that he should put faith in their connection.

"Do you want to look at the other places we were going to see?" he asked her. Instantly he saw her shriek, laugh and throw her arms around his neck.

"You are saying yes, right? About us living together … wherever we end up?" Cat asked.

Tom nodded and gave her a smile that made her feel like she could happily climb on his lap right then and…

"How is your decision making going?" they heard the agent ask as she returned to the yard.

"I think … we will … take it?" Tom asked Cat to be certain, but he was already fairly sure what she was thinking.

"Yes, I think we should. Where do we sign?"

~ ~ ~

"Finally getting a place of your own, huh? Aww, my brother is finally growing up," Graham teased Tom that night when he and Tessa visited the family home for dinner. He turned his attention to Cat. "Don't let him cook you anything though," he said in a mock whisper, resulting in the receipt of a light punch on his arm from his brother.

"Don't listen to him, Cat," Tessa said, giving Graham a good eye roll. "Graham can't cook and I haven't suffered from that yet. In fact, he makes a very good dishwasher!"

Tom looked at his mother, Victoria, sitting on the other side of him. When she caught him looking at her, she spoke.

"I'm proud of you both, you boys. No matter what your father is like, you two have the true Santini blood running through you. You are good men, and you will both be good fathers yourselves," she said, making Tom splutter the drink he'd been enjoying as she spoke.

"Only Tessa is pregnant, Mom," he said quietly and then looked directly at Cat. "Right?"

Seeing an opportunity to tease him and make him sweat a little, Cat kept him waiting, watching his face as she was silent before she laughed. "Right."

"Oh, yes, for now, but children will come," his mother replied. "Always, the Santinis have been a large family. Only your father went against the grain of the family honor and traditions, but you two will pick up where he caused a dent in the chain and you will straighten it out again. You have cousins aplenty here in Australia and many, many more in America. Make contact with those you don't already know, and get to know them. Feel the pride of being a Santini."

"But Mom, you weren't a Santini. Why do you sing their praises so highly?" Graham asked, wondering how she could speak so well of the family when her husband treated her so badly.

Victoria laughed. "But I *am* a Santini, my dear boy. Your father and I are second cousins. His family are my family, even though we are related distantly. We are both descendants of the same great grandparents."

As she finished speaking, she looked around all four faces at the table with her and saw surprised looks on each of them. She chuckled softly to herself. "I know more about the Santini family as a whole than you might expect. And certainly more than your father will know, I can promise you that! He never embraced the family he was part of. He always just wanted to run away and be anything *but* a Santini. No, now the family will grow through you two."

Everyone was silent for a long while, processing the news that no-one had heard before. In Tom and Graham, a new sense of pride began to grow.

~ ~ ~

Two weeks later, when Tom and Cat both had days off from their jobs, moving day finally came.

"It's a bit bare, isn't it?" Cat said as the stood in

their living area and looked around. Victoria had given them a wide range of household things to help them out as a start.

"Hmm, well, actually I like it. I mean we have this sofa here," he said, nudging her in that direction and gently guiding her down onto it before kissing her deeply. Then he was standing up and pulling her up with him and guiding her to the bedroom. "And we have this big bed here," he said, again nudging her down to deliver her a delightfully passionate kiss. One more maneuver and he had guided her into the kitchen. "And then we have this very sturdy table…"

In response to his remark, she laughed out loud. "Well, I am very glad that we have so much useful furniture."

Tom grinned at her as she pushed herself against him. With her arms wrapping around him, he leaned down and kissed her again and immediately she felt him pressing hard against her. She moaned in response. They hadn't been anywhere alone for two weeks at least, and she was hungry for him. Together they indulged in kissing deeply, tongues wrapping around one another as Tom felt himself stretched so much he thought he might burst at any moment.

"Hello?" they heard Graham call out.

Tom pulled away from Cat sharply as they both laughed. Tom moved quickly to the bathroom to let himself settle a bit before he had to face his brother. The move left Cat chuckling slightly as Graham and Tessa came into view.

"The front door was open. I hope it's okay for us to just walk in," Tessa said in response to the look - and blush - on Cat's face. "We aren't interrupting, are we?"

Cat smiled as if guilty of having been caught stealing a cookie from the cookie jar.

"No, nothing. Tom isn't far away. How about I get us drinks? What would you like?"

Tessa gave a smile that said she thought perhaps she and Graham had interrupted something but said nothing about that. "Oh no, I am fine, thanks. We just went out for lunch so I'm good."

Graham looked around and then let his gaze fall back to Cat. "Where's Tom?"

"Right here," his deep voice came from behind them all. "How's things?" he asked, appearing completely composed.

"We just wanted to drop off your housewarming gift," Graham said, lifting a large hamper onto the kitchen table. "This is for Cat, in case you mess up the cooking, Tom."

Cat laughed as she looked inside the hamper and saw all sorts of foods.

"Haha, you're a real blast," Tom said. "I suppose you want a tour."

The two men headed through the house while Cat turned to Tessa.

"Come outside. There's a swing seat among the bushes and fruit trees and the smell of the garden is divine."

Once they were settled, Tessa faced Cat. "How are you feeling? You know, about living with Tom full time?"

"I feel good," Cat replied, grinning. "I do love being with him, Tessa. I know it hasn't been very long that we've been together, but I do feel like … I don't know … like it's meant to be? It sounds soppy, doesn't it."

"No! I don't think it's soppy at all. Not when you really feel it and I believe that you do, and that Tom does too. I see the way he looks at you, Cat. He's looked at you like that right from the first day he saw you," she said and chuckled. "Do you remember? It was in the café. When you handed him back his scarf, the way he was looking at you then … that was hot!"

Cat laughed and cringed at the same time, thinking back to that day. Tessa had seen Cat when she had changed into more acceptable clothing, of course, so at least she didn't know about the first half of that day, when Tom had first set eyes on a very wet Cat.

"But how are you?" Cat asked, desperate to deflect the conversation. "How are you feeling?"

"Oh, I'm fine. Six months down, three months to go. All seems good, I think."

"And Graham? How is he with the pregnancy?"

"Protective!" Tessa answered, laughing softly. "I think he's happy. He seems happy anyway. He wants us to move out of my apartment but I've told him we can wait for that. The baby won't need its own bedroom for a long while, and even when it does, the small room that is my craft room at the moment will be perfectly fine. Of course, when I'm hearing crying every night I might rethink that decision."

"Well, if you need anything, I'm here," Cat said.

"Thank you."

~ ~ ~

"Are you nervous?" Graham asked Tom as they sat down on the sofa inside.

"No. Why? Should I be?"

"You haven't had a serious girlfriend before, Tom."

Tom nodded and smiled sadly. "I know, but it feels right and I couldn't live at home forever. I *am* 28 years old!"

"That isn't exactly a good reason to move in with someone."

"What? Don't be ridiculous, Graham! That isn't why I've moved here with Cat. We're living together because we love being together. And because I think she's amazing and beautiful, and just … incredible."

Graham smiled and slapped his brother on the back. "Good. Now where are the girls?" he said, standing up as Tom realized he had just fallen for his brother's teasing.

CHAPTER 10

Lying together that first night, after sufficiently testing the sofa, bed and kitchen table out for desired sturdiness, Cat and Tom smiled at each other.

"I think we have been blessed to have been given such well-built furniture. I hope it serves us well long into the future," Cat said, giggling like she was much younger than her years. It had taken a while but now Tom believed she had truly found peace and happiness once more. He didn't expect her to forget Tony. He only hoped that day to day she could keep moving forward with joy in her own life - her *new* life with him.

"I agree, although that table might need far more testing," Tom teased. "We didn't test it from all angles, after all. We must put that on the to-do list."

Cat giggled more. She felt elated but with every level of elation, she felt she half expected something bad to happen. Could she really be this happy? It had long felt like that just wasn't allowed. Not for her. As she heard those thoughts pass through her mind, she felt her emotions become mixed up. A moment later she couldn't distinguish between tears of happiness and tears of fear of what was to come.

Tom watched her face change and pulled her tightly against him. Most of the time she seemed happy but he expected that now and then this would happen. He sometimes felt overwhelmed too, at that stark reality of what had been before and what was now. It could be extremely overpowering. It was like something felt so good that it must be wrong, or there must be something bad to follow it.

Cat settled against him, gathering strength from him. It was irrational that she should feel like she did in that moment when only a short time earlier she had been in the heights of happiness. It wasn't logical but Tom didn't tease her about it. He did what she needed. He just held her. She didn't try to hold anything back. From much experience, she knew that when it was time to cry, it was time to cry. It was better to let it all out. After that, she always felt much more relaxed and able to move forward again.

Listening to her sob was difficult but Tom remained still and quiet, understanding the need to let go. After a long while, the sobs stopped and he saw her look at him.

"Thank you," she said softly as she attempted to give him a smile.

He kissed her before replying. "I'm always here,

Cat. You never have to pretend with me. Always just be yourself. When the sad times come, let them. Don't hide them."

"And does that apply to you too?" she asked "I know you have had moments of thinking about your past, Tom. Why do *you* never let go?"

He smiled at her sadly. "I wish I could, and one day I hope I will. For me, it's been a really long time since that mistake happened. Almost straight away after that, I was put in prison and I quickly learned that it wasn't a good idea to cry there! It's inside of me. One day it will release. When it does, don't worry, you'll know. I won't hide it from you either."

CHAPTER 11

A Month Later

Tom carefully removed the spent flower buds from the plants in the back garden. He'd never taken any time to learn about nature in the past but he was determined to maintain his commitment to the responsibility that came with renting the small cottage that had become his home.

Home. It was a nice word and for the first time in his life, he was living somewhere that truly felt like it was full of love. For one month they had been living together and for the most part, it had been only happy. Amongst all that happiness, Cat had let herself feel depths of her emotions twice more, falling into Tom's arms as the tears flowed. The last time had been two weeks ago. Tom suspected it might take a while longer for her to consistently allow herself to be happy, but he did believe it was coming. She deserved to be loved. She *knew* she deserved to be loved. She just had to now fully let herself *believe* it.

The air was changing. He wondered if he would have noticed something like that if he hadn't spent ten years locked away from the outside world. He stood up straight and looked around. The slow progression from summer to autumn made it more difficult to keep up with maintaining a tidy yard as the flowers wilted and the leaves persisted in falling but he loved it. Still working at the café five days out of seven, the garden was his second job but it didn't feel like a job or a chore. It felt like therapy. It was a time to let his mind be completely at rest and appreciate how his life was so changed since he'd been released from prison.

His attention was pulled from his thoughts as he felt his phone vibrating in his pocket. Pulling it out, he saw Graham's name appear on the screen.

"It's a perfect surf day," Tom heard his brother say when he'd answered. "Let's go."

Tom laughed but found himself adequately enticed. "Okay."

That was all he had to say, being as communicative as they were as brothers.

"We'll be there soon," Graham replied and hung up. No beating around the bush with his brother, Tom thought to himself.

He wandered into the small home and found Cat baking in the kitchen. She had never tried it before a week ago. Now she was on a baking frenzy. Tom found it amusing and adequately teased her but she didn't mind. She was finding a new passion … and enjoying eating it.

As he approached her, he saw she seemed to

have touched her hair with floury hands. He smiled at her. She was a sight, but a beautiful one all the same.

Cat watched as he moved toward her, his face alight with a combination of desire and contained laughter. He leaned down and kissed her softly before reaching one hand into her hair and trying to shake it free of the flour that sat there.

"Graham is coming over to take me surfing and I think Tessa is coming to visit you. Unless you want to come out surfing too?" he asked.

Cat heard the invitation and smiled at him. They had been out on surfboards together a few times since that first attempt but they both knew she wasn't really into it. It was nice sitting on the board out beyond the waves, in peace and solitude, but she had no desire to actually surf.

"No, that is your time with your brother. Besides, Tessa and I will have loads of girl talk to catch up on."

Tom pulled her to him and kissed her deeply. Cat happily wrapped her arms around him and blissfully shared her floury hands as she ran them through his hair. When she stepped away she contained the smile on her face as she noticed she'd done a pretty good job of sharing with him.

The knock on the door a few minutes later pulled Tom away from her completely. When he opened it, he was confronted with an amused

Tessa, even though she said nothing. It wasn't until Graham saw him that he realized what had happened.

"Do you have … cookie dough in your hair?" he asked, reaching forward to touch something in his brother's hair.

Tom laughed and shook his head vigorously to loosen whatever Cat had put in there. He was usually better at knowing when she did things like that but she'd got him good that time. Must have been that searing kiss, distracting him.

"Come on then," Graham said, watching his brother make movements similar to a wet dog shaking water off itself after having a swim. "You can share your cookie dough with the fish."

Tom walked back to the kitchen and kissed Cat softly and then grinned at her as if to say 'I'll get you back later'. Her body was instantly alert in anticipation.

Once the men had left, Tessa settled herself at the kitchen table.

"Those smell divine, Cat. What are you baking today?"

"Just chocolate chip and almond cookies today," Cat replied. "How are you feeling? I think you are larger every time I see you now."

"Oh, I know! And I have two more months to go yet. I already feel like I'm an elephant."

Cat giggled. "Well, you certainly don't look like

an elephant! You are glowing. I bet Graham finds it hard to keep his hands to himself with you looking so good."

Tessa smiled. "He *has* to keep his hands to himself now. I've laid down the rule. My hormones are on overload so it's the only way I can get through the days, keeping a slight distance from him. If I didn't put my foot down, he'd never be able to leave the house."

Cat giggled. "I'm sure he wouldn't object to that!"

~ ~ ~

Out on the water, Tom and Graham sat on their boards, talking while waiting.

"Are you happy, baby brother?" Graham asked Tom. Most of the time he forgot about Tom's previous life over that decade. Now and then he found himself wondering how he was really coping, being on the outside again.

"I am," Tom replied. "Very. Actually, I'm thinking about proposing to Cat."

Graham looked at him as if he were stunned.

"You don't think that's a good idea?" Tom asked, slightly unnerved by his brother's reaction.

Graham realized he hadn't looked as happy as he did feel at the news, and grinned. "On the contrary. That girl has had your heart for ages now. When will the big day be?"

"Well, I haven't asked her yet. She might say

no…"

"Tom, there is no way she's going to say no! I've seen the way she looks at you. She loves you. Why … how could you possibly doubt that?"

Tom smiled. He thought he was right in how Cat felt about him but he wouldn't know until he asked her. "I don't know. I guess we'll see when I ask."

"It will be fine," Graham reassured him.

"You have bigger things coming up. Only two months, is it?"

"It is. Well, seven weeks, the doctor said. I didn't know I wanted to have any kids but the closer this gets, the more I feel like I'm ready. I want to be a dad. And I want to be a *good* dad."

"You *will* be a good dad. Lord knows you and I have first-hand experience at what a good father *isn't* like!"

"I hope so. I don't want my child to feel like *I* have all my life…"

~ ~ ~

Later that night, sitting on the sofa in their small living area, Cat felt relaxed. She'd spent a good few hours chatting about anything and everything with Tessa. It had left her with a simple feeling of light-hearted happiness. She didn't know why fate had finally brought such good people into her life but she was extremely thankful that it had. She'd been on her own for so long before then, not knowing who to trust. These people, she put full trust in … full trust and full faith that they wouldn't hurt her.

She saw Tom come in and sit down beside her before he asked her about her afternoon. When she talked to him, nothing seemed too trivial. Whether she said important things or unimportant things, he always listened as if everything were of great importance. It helped her to be open about everything.

"How was your surf session with Graham?" she asked after she'd assured him she was happy.

"It was good, although we might have talked much more than we actually surfed. But it was good to have that time with him. He did remind me of an idea that came to me recently, though. I had been trying to not forget it but put it off for a while longer, but I think the time is right now," he said cryptically, causing a sliver of fretfulness in her.

Cat watched as he slid onto the floor in front of her and pulled out a small box from his pocket.

"Cat Cullen, I absolutely love and adore you, and I want to keep doing that for the rest of my life," he started to say and immediately heard a deep exhale from her. "You have amazing strength and you know how much you turn my legs to jelly," he continued and saw her smile as her eyes started to water. "Will you marry me?"

She sat forward on the edge of the sofa, lost for words. There was a beautiful, kind and loving man kneeling before her, proposing to her. It wasn't her first proposal but it affected her as if it were. She leaned close to him and brought her hands up to his face, cupping his jaw before kissing him softly.

"Tom Santini, you are the most incredible man I have ever met. Of course I am going to say yes. Do you think I'm crazy?!"

"So … that's a yes then?" he teased her, grinning widely.

She nodded and kissed him again. "Absolutely."

CHAPTER 12

Another Month Later

"The countdown is on, huh? Three more months and you will be Mrs Tom Santini. Oh! I am so excited for you!" Tessa exclaimed to Cat as they enjoyed a lunch out, away from their guys.

"Thank you, Tessa," Cat said, grinning. "But you are going through something even more amazing. You are going to give life to a human being. I don't think a wedding comes anywhere close to that miracle!"

Tessa laughed softly. All morning she had been experiencing slightly different feelings to normal. They left her aware of them, but not alarmed. She was in her eighth month of pregnancy. She expected her body would start feeling very strange in the coming weeks. Today she wanted to be happy for Cat.

The two women continued to chat until Tessa then felt a sharper tug in her belly. That one, she couldn't hide.

"Tessa! What is it?"

"I don't know," she said as she crumpled over slightly.

"We have to get you to the hospital … right?"

Cat asked, not knowing what had to be done, or when. "Come on, I'll get us a taxi."

Soon the two women were arriving at the hospital. In the delivery ward, Cat watched as Tessa was led off by a nurse.

"Call Graham!" she heard Tessa call out to her, jolting Cat to pull out her phone. Not having Graham's number, Tom was going to have to do. She hated calling him at work but felt she had no real choice.

"Hey, my lovely Foxy Cat. What's up?"

"Graham."

"What?" he asked, alarm evident in his voice. "What's happened to him?"

Cat shook her head. Of course he would assume she meant something had happened to Graham if she only said his name!

"Sorry, no. I'm at the hospital with Tessa. Can you call Graham and tell him to come here? We're up on the fourth floor."

There was silence before he seemed to comprehend what she was saying.

"Right! I'm on it. I'll call him right now," he said. "Chat to you later."

Tom looked at Toby and smiled apologetically. "Sorry to use my phone, Toby. Tessa's at the hospital. I just need to let my brother know."

Toby beamed. "It is time? Already? Oh my, I must prepare her something special and take it to her."

Tom laughed as he dialed his brother's number. "She might not be in the mood for food right now," he said to Toby just as his call went to Graham's voicemail. "Graham, Cat is at the hospital right now with Tessa. Drop what you're doing and get down there. I'll come down when my shift is finished at six … oh, they are on the fifth floor. No, wait. Maybe it was the fourth floor. I'm not sure. Sorry. I'll see you there."

~ ~ ~

Cat sat in the waiting room closest to where Tessa had disappeared behind large swinging doors. No-one had turned up. Not Graham. Not Tom. She wondered how she might get in touch with anyone from Tessa's family. She'd never met or even seen any of them even though she'd heard stories about them from Tessa. Now she wished she'd had the foresight to ask Tessa for a contact number for someone … *anyone* … in her family. Cat was so used to being on her own that sometimes she forgot that other people had parents, brothers, sisters, cousins…

And what about Victoria? She would want to be there if something were happening to her grandchild. She supposed that was a decision for Graham to make. But where was he?

"Who is here for Mrs Tessa Santini?" she heard a woman's voice call out to the waiting room.

"I am," Cat responded, seeing that no-one else was there yet. "I am a friend of hers."

"She's in labor…"

"Isn't it too soon?" Cat asked, horrified at the thought of anything happening to the little Santini due to make its arrival in the world.

The doctor smiled at her. "It is a month earlier than expected but we will do everything we can to make the delivery a successful one. Are there family that will be coming?"

Cat nodded. "I have passed on the news that Tessa is here and that should be reaching her husband. I don't know about family on her side. Am I able to see her, and ask her if she wants someone to come in?"

The doctor nodded and led her to a small room with a bed, two chairs and a large square bath in the corner. The look on Tessa's face was intense, like she was directly amid great pain. Cat didn't know what to do. All she could do was watch as Tessa let out a long and loud scream. When that seemed to be over, all she could do was wait until finally Tessa quietened and seemed to see Cat there.

"Cat, thanks for still being here. Where's Graham?"

"He's on his way," Cat said, hoping that was the truth. "I can stay till he gets here. But Tessa, who do you want me to ring in your family?"

Tessa looked like she was gearing up for another expression of pain, but grabbed her phone from the side table and handed it to Cat. "Call my mother or father. They are named like that in there. If you can't get hold of them, try my sister Mary."

"Got it. Mom, Dad, Mary," Cat said as she scrolled through the contacts list. Just as she was about to dial, Tessa started to express her pain again. Cat crept out of the room, believing she probably wouldn't even be noticed as having left.

She dialed the first number and was relieved to hear Tessa's mother at the end of the line. That was easy. The news was given. Tessa's mother was coming. Now Cat had helped with that side of things.

"Where is she?" she heard Graham's voice call out. When he focused on her, she pointed to the room where Tessa lay. "Thanks, Cat," he said to her in passing as he touched her arm with his hand.

Cat's work, it seemed, was done. She made herself comfortable in the waiting room, not sure if she should stay or not. The clock on the wall said it was 5pm. It would be a long while before Tom walked in, if that was his plan. She sat back, pulled her book from her bag, and settled in for a long wait.

After six, she felt Tom sit beside her before she

saw him.

"Is there any news? Is she alright?" he asked, a slight urgency in his voice.

Cat smiled at him. "As far as I know she's still in labor. I haven't heard that anything is going wrong in there. Graham is in there, and so is Tessa's mother."

Tom felt himself calm down and finally looked right at her before leaning closer and kissing her soft lips. He took her hand in his.

"I'm glad you were with her."

"Me too."

After another hour Graham came out, grinning. "I have a daughter. A beautiful baby girl," he said, obviously happy and proud.

Tom stood up and hugged him. They weren't generally a huggy type of family but this occasion seemed to deserve it. "And Tessa? Is she okay?"

"Yep. She's resting. I'm a father. You're an uncle," he said, absolutely beaming.

Tom and Cat both laughed. It was the most animated that Cat had seen Tom's brother since she had met him.

Graham left them and returned to the room, smiling all the way.

Tom turned to Cat. "Should we stay? Should we go?" he asked, uncertain what protocol was for such an occasion.

"Don't you want to meet your niece?"

"My niece," he said and chuckled softly. "Hey, I have a niece!"

Cat saw Tessa's mother come out. "Go in and meet the little one. She's adorable."

Tom smiled and thanked her before he and Cat walked into the room. Tessa was sitting up looking exhausted but happy. In her arms was a tiny bundle.

"Cat! Tom! Come and meet our daughter," she said, encouraging the two of them to move forward.

Tom looked down into the tiny face. "She's tiny."

The nurse heard the comment and spoke up. "She's a little early but she is fine. In literally a matter of days she will grow bigger. She's healthy. That's the main thing. Now, it is getting late and visiting hours are coming to an end. Dad, you can stay a little longer but I'll have to ask you two to leave and come back during visiting hours tomorrow. Anytime after ten is fine."

Cat heard the request so smiled and said goodbye to Graham and Tessa. Outside the door, she turned to Tom and could see wonder on his face. Nothing needed to be said as they made their way home, both in awe of the wonder of pregnancy and childbirth.

CHAPTER 13

Three Months Later

Tom looked in the mirror one more time. Today was his wedding day. For the first time in his life, he was wearing a suit. It was pale grey so seemed to accentuate his dark hair and dark eyes even more. It seemed a little too suave for him, but he looked okay. He was far more eager to see his bride.

"Yes, you look fine. Now stop posing in front of the mirror and let's get to the ceremony," Graham said, teasing his younger brother.

Tom smiled at him. He was nervous, but also excited. He and Cat had spent months together and he was sure he was doing the right thing. He briefly wondered if his father would attend the wedding. No enthusiasm had been shown to do so and Tom certainly didn't expect it. What his father thought of him and Graham, Tom had never known. All he really knew was that his father didn't seem to care about them at all. It was no wonder that already Graham was showering affection on his daughter. Both boys knew rejection. Neither would pass it on to anyone else.

The two of them made their way to the beach

where plastic chairs were lined up. It was a small crowd but everyone important was there. Both men moved forward, looking around the crowd that was seated, and saw everyone smiling. Their mother held pride of place, right at the front, in the seat closest to the makeshift altar.

Someone's phone started playing the wedding march. It was a meager effort and sound but everyone laughed at it. They had no desire to upset a public beach so needed nothing so loud as a proper sound system.

Once the music had begun Tom turned and saw Cat walking toward him. It was the first time he'd seen her dress. Strapless and pure white, it had a well-fitting, embroidered, corset-like bodice that showed her curves perfectly. He gulped. She was beautiful all the time, but in that moment she was absolutely breathtaking.

Cat watched his face as she walked forward with Tessa next to her. Having no family herself, it seemed fitting that Tessa play the role of the person who would give her away. It wasn't normal but it worked for them.

As she reached Tom, she looked at him. His smile was full of passion, making her blush. He liked it when she blushed. In fact, he liked it when she did anything.

The vows were spoken. The rings were exchanged. They were declared husband and wife.

Tom pulled her into his arms and kissed her like she deserved to be kissed. He would kiss her today and he would kiss her for all the days ahead.

The sound of everyone clapping and making wolf whistle sounds made them laugh as they broke apart and turned to face the crowd of people coming forward toward them. They moved around, making sure to talk to everyone.

"You finally did it, Cousin," Tom heard a voice say and when he turned around he saw his cousin, Daniel, standing and grinning at him. "Some lass finally secured the heart of Tom Santini." Tom looked at Daniel and rolled his eyes but smiled. He knew his cousin. They had spent time together growing up. Daniel was one of the few family members who had visited him fairly regularly throughout his decade in jail.

"Daniel! It is so good to see you. Thanks for coming. This is my wife, Cat," Tom said, introducing them while trying that new word on for size. Wife. Yes, he would definitely get used to saying that. "How are things with you?"

Daniel smiled at Cat and shook her hand before turning to face Tom again.

"I'm good, yeah. I'm heading over to the States in a couple of weeks to see Cameron and the other cousins there."

"Oh yeah? That sounds great. How long are you away for?"

"Only three weeks. I'm going to try and see everyone there and meet as many family members as I can. Then I'll be back again."

"Hey, Daniel!" they heard Graham's voice call out as he came closer to them and hugged his cousin. "I hear you're bound for the land of the City of Angels! Maybe to find a bride, huh?" Graham teased, making Daniel laugh.

"You never know, Graham. You just never know," he said mysteriously before he moved away from them.

"He's different, is our Daniel. But he's a Santini, as are we. He's family. And we do need all the family we can get, I am thinking."

It was a strange thing for Graham to have said but neither Tom or Cat replied as they watched him walk away, leaving them alone for the moment.

"Well, my beautiful bride, how would you like to take a small walk along the beach?"

Cat nodded and smiled at him before taking his hand in hers.

They walked until they were a distance away that they could have quiet. Together they sat down on the sand, neither caring about sand getting in their clothes. They leaned on each other and looked out to the horizon as the sun began to set.

"I love you, Mrs Santini," Tom said quietly, deeply and huskily, in a voice that was only ever intended to be heard by her.

Cat turned to look at him. He was such a handsome man, being so tall with his dark hair and dark eyes.

"I love you too, Mr Santini."

They leaned in, kissed, and found themselves blissfully happy. Their story was only just beginning. Many, many more chapters were yet to come.

~~~~~~~~~~~~~~~~~~

The End
~~~~~~~~~~~~~~~~~~